9/06

Teen.

D0396442

KIPLING'S CHOICE

KIPLING'S CHOICE

WRITTEN BY GEERT SPILLEBEEN
TRANSLATED BY TERESE EDELSTEIN

HOUGHTON MIFFLIN COMPANY

BOSTON 2005

www.houghtonmifflinbooks.com

The text of this book is set in Agenda and Dante.

Library of Congress Cataloging-in-Publication Data
Spillebeen, Geert.
[Kipling's Keuze English] Kipling's choice / written by Geert Spillebeen ;
translated by Terese Edelstein.   p. cm.
Summary: In 1915, mortally wounded in Loos, France, eighteen-year-old John Kipling,
son of writer Rudyard Kipling, remembers his boyhood and the events leading
to what is to be his first and last World War I battle.

ISBN 0-618-43124-1

1. Kipling, John, 1897-1915—Juvenile fiction. 2. Kipling, Rudyard, 1865-1936—Juvenile
fiction. [1. Kipling, John, 1897-1915—Fiction. 2. Kipling, Rudyard, 1865-1936—Fiction
3. Death—Fiction. 4. Loos, Battle of, Loos-en-Gohelle, France, 1915—Fiction.
5. World War, 1914-1918—France—Fiction. 6. Fathers and sons—Fiction. 7. War—Fiction.]
I. Edelstein, Terese. II. Title.
PZ7.S7549Ki 2005
[Fic]—dc22

                    2004020856

ISBN-13: 978-0618-43124-3

Interior design and composition by Pamela Consolazio

Manufactured in the United States of America
WOZ 10 9 8 7 6 5 4 3 2 1

KIPLING'S CHOICE

JOHN KIPLING GAZES WILDLY THROUGH THE THICK CIRCLES OF HIS DUSTY SPECTACLES. In the doorway one can clearly see how young and undeveloped this fierce little officer still is. Panting, he shoves open the splintered door against the outside wall. John Kipling hops on one leg and lets himself fall against the house, looking for support on the partially destroyed windowsill. A final sharp bang shudders through the stone house.

A few minutes earlier, under cover of fire, four men, with Kipling in the lead, stealthily crept toward the isolated building. Kipling crawled to a spot under the window of a machine-gun nest and wiped it out with a well-aimed hand grenade. Sergeant Cochrane and two of his men then stormed inside.

"Surely twenty Germans were in this nest, sir," a voice calls from inside. Bowing his head, Sergeant Cochrane comes out through the doorway. The two soldiers follow him.

"You're wounded, Sergeant," Kipling remarks when he sees Cochrane's bloodstained shoulder. He speaks as if he were calling attention to a speck of lint on the Sergeant's sleeve.

"That leg of yours looks worse than my shoulder, Lieutenant."

Kipling glances down at his khaki trouser leg, which is glistening dark red from his knee to the puttee above his shoe. "Has that machine-gun nest been put out of action, Sergeant?" he asks.

"It's completely destroyed, sir."

Cochrane speaks to his superior in a respectful tone, for Kipling's first hours in the line of fire have made quite an impression. In the few weeks that he has served as lieutenant, this youngest officer in the Irish Guards has been under close scrutiny by his chiefs and foot soldiers alike. It's no wonder. Everyone knows Kipling. Rudyard Kipling, of course, is his father, his "Daddo," as John calls him. Everyone knows at least one of his father's books or exciting stories, especially *The Jungle Book* or *Kim*. Most can even rattle off a couple of Kipling's verses from memory. But John wants to establish himself on his own merit. He bends over backward for his "boys." They are all older than he is, but at the front they're equally green.

"Twenty-five, Sergeant," John Kipling says. He points his thumb over his shoulder to the inside of the building. "Twenty-five Fritzes, not twenty, as you said."

"But now they're all the best kind of Germans—stone dead," Sergeant Cochrane chortles.

A shell lands in the chalk pit behind the house they are leaning against, splitting the pit in two. Rubble and glowing shrapnel from the exploded shell pierce through the back wall and the roof. Cochrane and his two men duck down.

"No time to lose, chaps," says Lieutenant Kipling. He blows the grit from his trim little mustache and jumps up on his good leg.

This much good luck is bound to run out, Sergeant Cochrane thinks, shaking his head. Half an hour earlier he begged Kipling to take cover next to him behind a sandbag of a captured trench. When enemy machine guns began to plow a groove into the ground between the house and their own position, he finally grabbed his

3

young officer by the sleeve with a "Sorry, sir" and pulled him down. A moment later the bullets hit the sandbag behind their heads. "Quite warm here, isn't it, Sergeant?" was Kipling's sarcastic comment.

"Come on, boys!" John calls, waving toward the trench. Twenty heads, which had invisibly been following their officer's every move, emerge from the ground. "Come on, boys!" he shouts again and again, pistol in the air, as he limps behind the right side of the house. The shouting is now taken up by his men in the lead, who are storming across the open terrain toward the chalk pit like a ribbon waving in the wind.

Shouting makes you forget, shouting numbs your fear, shouting blocks your ears from the din of the oncoming shells and the whistling bullets, from the wails of the boy next to you who can't move any farther because his legs are gone or because his intestines are lying at his feet, his belly ripped open by flying shrapnel and scalding-hot lead balls from fragmentation bombs.

John Kipling has waited months for this glorious moment, and he has waited with great patience. At first nobody wanted him in their ranks, this filthy-rich kid, this sickly dandy. Too slow for a military career, dragged along on Papa's long arm because of his extreme near-sightedness, and then too young for the front . . .

Dragging his injured foot with difficulty, Lieutenant Kipling pumps his good leg with his hand on his knee and proceeds at least fifty meters farther. The adrenaline in his blood blocks out the pain in his head.

"Come on, boys!"

The troops wrestle with their heavy packs. A sudden burst of artillery fire scatters the platoon in all directions. Caps fly through the air, soldiers stumble, then pick up their guns and try to stand up. More and more boys fall behind, as helpless as children whimpering for their mothers. Some lie there, surprised and speechless; others are convulsing, twitching, dying. A few are already motionless.

John Kipling hesitates, but the sergeants below blow their whistles and get most of the boys back in one line. "Come on!" John calls encouragingly, and with his pistol he points in the direction of the chalk pit.

That boy will be given a Victoria Cross, Sergeant Cochrane thinks when he sees his lieutenant in action. And on his first day, too!

Cochrane and the other two Irish Guards crouch down and stumble over to their officer. One by one they sink down to the warm grass, exhausted. A road runs between the chalk pit and a wooded area. Everyone assumes that Kipling will gather his platoon together so that the men can give each other cover while crossing the road. Perhaps he will ask the artillery to fire a few rounds into the woods first.

"Quarter to five. This is proceeding too slowly," the slender lieutenant growls. He stands up straight and snaps his pocket watch shut. It is a gift his father brought back from Switzerland, a watch with the initials J.K. engraved upon it.

A new wave of shells rains over their heads and plunges with a devilish din into the dry, chalky soil. Fountains of white dust and black smoke cloud the horizon. Heavy machine-gun fire, which comes from the bushes higher up, just past the road, drowns out the moans of the wounded.

Lying on his stomach, Sergeant Cochrane peers into the line of fire. The other platoons are progressing even more slowly than his.

"Gas! Gas, Lieutenant!" Cochrane screams, pointing to the poisonous green cloud ahead, above the position of the Scots Guards.

"No danger yet, Sergeant," Kipling calls back. "The wind is in our favor."

"Shouldn't you seek better cover, sir?" asks the sergeant hesitantly.

"How would my men know where to proceed then?" he answers impatiently.

Those are the last words exchanged by the two men.

"Come on, boys!" Kipling shouts as he runs limping in the direction of the woods, toward the enemy. Cochrane runs after him. A little later the sergeant is dragged out of the trees, half-dead, overcome by poison gas.

At five o'clock Lieutenant John Kipling is observed for the last time. His head is bloodied and he seems half-crazy, bawling from the pain. He is stumbling, falling, and rolling over the thin, pale earth. He takes a bandage and tries to stop the blood that is gushing from the shattered remains of his mouth, but blood is spurting just as fast from a gash in his neck. Thick drops penetrate deep into the dry, chalky soil of the Bois Hugo in northern France, between the villages of Hulluch and Loos.

It is Monday, September 27, 1915. John Kipling turned eighteen just six weeks ago. He is screaming from terror and pain, screams that are high as a child's and just as piercing. None of the bewildered soldiers dare to help him, for fear of humiliating the young officer.

In the confusion of the shells smashing all around, each man runs for his life. The shrieking, damaged face of this normally friendly lieutenant emits only animal sounds, but his cries are swallowed up by the noise of his very first field battle. And his very last, as well.

■ ■ ■

Though John Kipling literally feels his life dripping away through his fingers and is in agonizing pain, he wants to maintain his dignity. Daddo would want that, too. Above all else he is an officer, a gentleman. He has the same feeling of embarrassment as he did when he walked into the office of the assistant headmaster, stumbled over the carpet, and fell flat on his face. He was eleven and attending boarding school in Rottingdean.

"Embracing Mother Earth, John Kipling?" the assistant headmaster asked.

"No sir, kissing Cousin Carpet."

■ ■ ■

Daddo had a good laugh about it later. But John can't save himself with a witty remark this time. This situation is deadly serious.

God! This is unbearable, this pain! It must have been shrapnel, a shell fragment. My spectacles, my pince-nez! Without my spectacles I'm nothing . . .

"We'll pull you through. Those eyes will be all right," Rudyard Kipling wrote to his son more than once. He knows what he is talking about, for he himself has been wearing glasses since childhood. They called him "Gigger" as a child, "Ruddy Giglamps." Everyone can draw a caricature of this brand-new Nobel Prize winner: a walrus mustache, two jam-jar lids for eyes, and a pipe.

Saint Aubyns Prep School. John has just turned ten. He arrives on September 1 in a uniform that is stiffly starched and ironed. An expensive boarding school, of course. They ride there in style, in Daddo's chauffeur-driven Rolls-Royce. Mummy has stayed home with Elsie, John's older sister. Rudyard and John survey the whole building, the two of them, father and son. The distinguished, famous Mr. Kipling and his slender little son in his new school uniform.

"You're going hunting alone in the jungle now, Mowgli," the father says. He grasps his son firmly by the hand.

"I'm not a tenderfoot anymore, am I, Akela?"

"Keep your chin up, fellow."

Rudyard Kipling has never had to leave his son alone before, but he doesn't let on about it. He has big plans for John. The navy, at the very least. His own childhood dream.

They write to each other twice a week, just as they promised. Sometimes Daddo's letters come from the most exotic places on earth. One even comes from the fancy VIP railway carriage in which the celebrated English writer travels as he gives readings throughout Canada. John devours the reports about the spouting whales between Victoria and Vancouver, and of the royal reception his father gets wherever he goes. John writes back and maintains a brave front, with not a word about the terrible homesickness for Bateman's, their country house near the village of Burwash, in southern England.

Once John writes about the ghost hunt. Beresford, the boy who sleeps next to John in the dormitory, lay in bed and was shaking with fear, for he thought he saw ghosts roaming through the house. In the dead of night John pulled on his sturdy shoes and crept down below, lantern in hand, to calm poor Beresford.

"Good boy!" his father writes back. "That's what any man wanting to join the navy would do. I'll bring you back a Hunter pocket watch. It's made of gunmetal and comes with a brown leather watchguard . . ." John is then eleven years old.

■ ■ ■

Oh God, help me! Make it stop! He would like to cry out, but his crushed palate spews only unintelligible, animal moans. The bandage he holds over his mouth is full of splinters from his jawbone. *My eyes!* he wants to shout. Thick red drops drip down his forehead, over his eyelashes. He falls forward and rolls onto his side. In his panicked state he is unable to determine exactly where he has been hit. The pain is tearing through his whole body. Lieutenant Kipling is especially worried about his eyes. Just as always, ever since his childhood.

■ ■ ■

He has just turned fourteen. The specialist in Switzerland gives the Kiplings little hope. John's loss of vision is getting worse each year. At home he begins to wear glasses every now and then. Daddo might as well forget about planning a naval career for his son. John will now attend the Wellington School, which is geared toward preparing its students for a future life in the army.

"Your eyes, boy, how can I explain it?" Rudyard says and sucks on his mustache. They are sitting on the cedar bench next to the rectangular pond that lies behind Bateman's, their country house. The lichen-covered stone trim forms a perfect border around the water. The splashing of the classic Greek fountain in the middle of the pond makes the silence bearable.

"There are still possibilities in the army," says Daddo despondently. He moves a little closer to John. "I know what you're feeling, boy. I have the same eyes, you know. I had the same dreams of the navy."

John feels worse for his father than for himself. He pushes his silver-rimmed spectacles farther up his nose, shrugs his shoulders, and gently takes his father by the arm. "So, I am really a bit like you, Daddo," he says with a sigh.

The great writer, never at a loss for words, can only swallow and stare at the white water lilies. Father and son sit quietly for a while. Then they look at each other; the one pair of spectacles reflects the other. Hand in hand they walk under the pergola to the pasture behind the variegated brick wall. They follow the Dudwell River to a remote corner by the old water mill. It is at this favorite hideout that the father tells his son stories about his own childhood days in India, stories that he simply cannot put down on paper.

John's eyes occasion regular visits to the best specialists in Switzerland. These trips also serve as fantastic holidays every winter. The Kiplings regularly go to the ski resort at Engelberg, where young John has great fun with Oscar Hornung. The novelist E.W. Hornung does not live too far from Burwash and the Hornungs also travel to Switzerland each year for winter sports. John and Oscar become best friends. Oscar is overwhelmed the first time he meets the great Kipling; he has such admiration for his hero, this writer of *The Jungle Book* and all those other fantastic stories, that he can hardly move. And John will never forget the time he visited Oscar's uncle, Arthur Conan Doyle, the creator of Sherlock Holmes.

Switzerland is always fun for John because Rudyard is so different from his usual self: he is not the stiff papa with the somber look and the black silk bowler hat, but a playful friend. When the weather is bad he makes up all kinds of silly games. The hotel in Engelberg is usually packed with celebrities from high society, strange creatures who provide an endless source of amusement for Oscar and John.

■　■　■

He can clearly hear himself scream; an icy, drawn-out cry, like a pig bleeding on the butchering block. He can also hear a sound like that of steam engines pounding in the bowels of a ship. Is the noise due to the searing pain? Or is it from the roaring of the artillery flying above the chalk pit?

■　■　■

"Turn that noise off! John, for the love of God, stop that record!"

Christmas 1911 is a glorious time. For days Bateman's has been buzzing with music.

"Oh, Daddo! A gramophone!"

Feelings are best kept to oneself, especially among men, yet it is clear to see that Daddo enjoys John's irrepressible hugs. John turned fourteen in the summer, and Wellington's military discipline has made him quieter. During these couple of weeks he nestles down in the warm cocoon of Bateman's with Mummy, Daddo, and Elsie.

Daddo cranks the machine and sets the needle on the record. John can easily hear the crackling amid the tense silence that precedes the first song, in perfect harmony with the crackling in the fireplace. Elsie puts her hands over her ears. Mummy, dubious, shrugs her shoulders. And with eyebrows dancing, Daddo sucks his pipe and winks mischievously at John, the apple of his eye.

Twenty-four fragile Bakelite phonograph records: songs by Harry Lauder, whom John and Daddo went to see recently at a London music hall; then the fairy-like Marie Lloyd (John clipped a rather revealing picture of her from a magazine and slipped it into his world atlas); the inevitable Caruso, singing the best of Verdi; and naturally a couple of recordings of military marches. John can't get enough of it. By the time he goes back to Wellington after the New Year, he has already gone through half a box of gramophone needles.

■ ■ ■

I lie on my back and feel nothing, hear nothing. There is, though, a big head dancing before my eyes. It has a cap on. Who is he? His face is black against the light gray sky. Have I fallen? His mouth won't be still. He is shouting at me and I feel like I'm watching a silent film. Why am I lying here?

John takes a serious fall around Easter 1913, the year he turns sixteen. His parents have just returned from Cairo. His sister, Elsie, has been in Paris with Miss Ponton, the governess. Everyone is back at Bateman's now. The children are on holiday.

"Isn't it fantastic?" Daddo says as he darts around the

shiny motorcycle like a little boy. He taps his pipe against his heel and stuffs it in his jacket pocket.

"A BSA 500 cc!" John can say no more.

His father swings his leg stiffly over the cycle. Both he and John are true motor fanatics. John is just as crazy about that green Rolls-Royce, the car Daddo rides around in everywhere. They call it the *Green Goblin*. For minutes at a time they can be amused by the *clickety-clack* of the valves when the chauffeur opens the hood for a routine check. And Rudyard has already ordered a new model, a Duchess.

John first takes his new motorcycle on a few turns right in front of the door, around Donkey Hill. But each day he ventures a bit farther. He wears a leather helmet with flaps and big goggles over his pince-nez. He roams across the border of Kent and East Sussex.

"Good practice for a future soldier," thinks Rudyard, who regards every application of modern technology as a terrific boost for the mighty army of the British Empire.

The first discreet complaints come in fairly quickly. When E. W. Hornung, Oscar's father, lets slip that John is scaring the living daylights out of quiet Burwash with his motorcycle and knocking over the startled villagers, Daddo chuckles, "That's my boy!" But he will have to speak to John about it.

He is too late. He is summoned to the neighboring village of Sissinghurst. A farmer fished John out of a ditch, thinking the boy was dead, and carried him along on his horse cart. Bruises, numerous scratches, a mild concussion, according to the doctor. And a sleeve torn off his leather motor jacket. The BSA is stuck in a hawthorn hedge, the frame and wheels damaged beyond repair. The engine, still purring, is hanging in the fresh greenery of the bushes.

"Reliable machines," exclaim John and Daddo, and they laugh about it afterward.

"The engine is still running," John tries to mutter to the dark face above his head, but he only manages to blow red bubbles through his shattered nose. As he regains consciousness, the excruciating pain creeps into his shaken body, cruel as a knife under the fingernails. The man in the cap is startled by the scream that resounds from the quivering mouth of the little officer.

John tries to concentrate on his glasses. With one

hand he fitfully searches his breast pocket for the chain of the pince-nez, the silver nose clip. *Daddo said . . .* He feels the shadowy silhouette above him take away his officer's pistol, for that hangs on a string around his neck, too. Suddenly he hears a voice, snatches of sentences, and the rattling of gunfire.

He knows that voice. It is his father's.

"Of course, the optician didn't design those glasses for diving and swimming, but when you're at school I want you to wear them as much as possible. Put them on a chain or a string; in that way you'll surely spare me the cost of a few pairs."

The pince-nez can't boost his school results. The motorbike, the ultimate bribe, can't help his performance either. By summer John even threatens to quit Wellington.

His bloodied fingers feel the twisted frames. There is still a piece of glass in them.

"It's not so bad if you break a pair." Daddo's voice sounds clear now. "Wear them as much as you can, boy!"

"Yes, Daddo."

"Read again! The second row from left to right. What are the letters?"

The man in the white coat and the pointer. . . . The eye test. . . .

"Let me go!" John wants to shout. But only meaningless gibberish comes from his crushed larynx.

"Sorry, Mr. Kipling, but this won't suffice for the army."

It is May 1913 and the upcoming exams at Wellington weigh like a block of concrete on John's shoulders.

Daddo has had a squash court installed at Bateman's ("After all, officers play squash"), and he promises John a new motorcycle.

"I can't take it anymore," John sobs. But the silhouette can't understand the words.

■　■　■

The pain disappears. Not entirely. Oh yes, please let it stay like this! It's bad enough, but at least I can stand it.

Have I been taken away? Why is it so quiet all of a sudden? The shooting has stopped. Voices are crying in the distance. Many wounded. Is there no one to take over the command? This can't be. Attack, boys!

Two hands on my arm, and two more on my side. They pull and push me. I hear them count: "One, two, three! Lift!"

And again: "One, two, three!"

"No, Master John, like this. Look, first your left foot forward, then swing your right leg back."

He tries slowly: one, two, three. A tango is very sexy when you try it in slow motion. He grasps Miss Malone firmly around her middle and furtively sniffs her delicate perfume when she leans against him. She leads him superbly: one, two, three . . .

Ooow! Bastards! Why don't they just let me lie on my back?

"One, two, three, and hup!"

"Good, Master John." Miss Malone is the nicer of the two dance teachers. He loves her voice. Elsie practices with Miss Pratt. It is October 1913. The whole house is buzzing with the tangos played on his gramophone. John is barely sixteen. Innocent, his mother thinks. Otherwise she would certainly not have Miss Malone come to Bateman's. He enjoys the tango lessons.

"Master John has a remarkable talent," his teacher says.

But not for dancing, John thinks.

The summer is spent doing math assignments, but eventually John is promoted to the next form at Wellington, by the skin of his teeth. They already know that Engelberg will be a math review as well as a ski holiday. Miss Ponton, the governess, must work on his math skills.

George Cecil, son of Lord Edward Cecil, comes to visit. He is dressed in the full regalia of his uniform from Sandhurst, the legendary officers' school. Daddo questions him endlessly about his military training. Of course John doesn't leave George's side for a moment, and listens to every word. He has probably sped by the majestic Sandhurst on his motorcycle ten times by now. God, how he envies George. With his mousy little glasses and small stature, John feels even more insignificant when he stands next to him.

"What a fine young man. He already looks like a real officer," Mummy muses a bit too emphatically.

"Precisely. He's completely Lord Edward," Daddo agrees.

John worries about his grades. Another year at Wellington. And then?

Clammy hands on my hot forehead. Someone gently dabbing the sweat on my face. Mummy? No, it's all blood. The ground is hard and cold, the grass is rustling.

Shells are whistling in the distance. A few seconds of silence.

Waiting for the rumbling as they come down. Voices right by my ear now.

"A bit of mint tea, boy."

Mummy, what are you doing here at the front? Is Daddo coming, too?

"Here, drink up."

A man's voice. Daddo?

"Better not, Sergeant. He won't make it. Besides, how would you put that bottle to his mouth? He has no mouth!"

An Irish accent. One of my men? Who are you? God! That pain again! No!

Restlessly the gravely wounded lieutenant shakes his bloodied head back and forth.

"He wants to say something," says the soldier next to him. The soldier sighs.

"How could he? God damn, what a mess," the sergeant curses.

"He's delirious."

"It won't be long now. We can't do anything for him."

John lies in bed. Mummy is sitting next to him. She has brought him some mint tea. It is spring 1914. The magnolias are in full bloom, and the sunlight on the flowers in the garden colors the walls of his room. It is already the third time this year that he has had to come home from school; he's been suffering from fever, nightmares, and just feeling sick. He wants to quit school. His grades are slipping again.

Daddo comes to comfort him. "Sandhurst isn't really

necessary, boy. We'll find something else. The King's Army has many doors."

John can hear the disappointment in his father's voice.

"Damned eyes." Daddo tries again. "It's not *your* fault, John."

At the beginning of May they decide to send him to Bournemouth for a cram course in the hopes of preparing him for the entrance exam to Oxford. John graduates from the course and everyone is relieved, at least for the time being. But the world is holding its breath. War breaks out on August 4. "The Great War, the war to end all wars!" claim the European heads of state.

Perfectly timed, Rudyard Kipling thinks. *This is John's chance.*

In two weeks I'll be seventeen, John Kipling thinks.

■   ■   ■

"Down, down, Sergeant!" a voice calls in panic.

Lieutenant Kipling is rudely awakened.

A familiar voice. But whose? Jesus, I feel absolutely nothing, as if my whole body was sleeping. The light goes on and off.

"We're getting the full load, Connelly. Down! Take cover!"

Ffwee–ee–ee. The earth spatters open in all directions.

God Almighty. Are the shells ours or the Germans'? How long have I been here? Here it comes, one is enough to bury me in one fell swoop or grind me up into a thousand pieces of meat.

John Kipling is completely paralyzed and continually bleeding from his head. Fragments of the hellish offensive overwhelm him now and then. The noise of the battle goes on and off as if someone were playing with the volume knob. Each time he passes out he is blown awake by thunderous noise that is as loud as every storm of his entire life all rolled into one. There are voices of fellows who crawl right by him. "This is—ugh—our lieutenant, the young Kipling!" "Poor devil."

How long ago is that now? Five minutes, five hours? Sometimes he is awakened by clumps of earth and lime which rain down on him.

The pain has become much less. Perhaps I'll make it, he wagers.

"See that? He's looking about," says an invisible voice.

John feels empty. With difficulty he squints to see who is sitting next to him. Everything is black.

"He's looking but he can't see anything," another voice answers.

John wants to protest.

"Left $\frac{6}{36}$ without glasses, $\frac{6}{6}$ with glasses." The voice is clear and emotionless.

The war is six days old. John has voluntarily reported to the Ministry of War in London. He wants to serve in Lord Kitchener's new army. Not wanting to pass up such a chance, he is now standing in line for the eye exam.

"Right $\frac{6}{36}$ without glasses, $\frac{6}{6}$ with." The verdict is given: "Unsatisfactory."

John grits his teeth to keep from talking back to the man.

"Perhaps you could report to a local recruiting office in your area," advises a friendly officer as John exits.

Disillusioned, John returns to Brown's Hotel, the London residence of the Kipling family. Rudyard and Carrie Kipling are upset by their son's tone of voice when they get him on the telephone, and they rush to

London in the *Green Goblin*. By the time they arrive, John has already left to see Colonel Feilden, a family friend, to lick his wounds.

"Next week you'll be seventeen, John. Maybe they'll be more accommodating then," suggests Daddo the next day. "Do you know what? We'll try together."

John lives on hope. On his birthday they ride in the Rolls to Hastings, then to Maidstone. When the recruiting sergeants and officers recognize Daddo, they bow like pocket knives and greet him with stiff salutes. But for the second time it's to no avail. Always those weak eyes . . .

"Maybe they don't want me as an officer, but do you think they'll take me as an ordinary soldier?" John muses with a sigh.

"Maybe, boy. Maybe."

"Maybe, Daddo? Is that all you can say? *Maybe?*" John asks reproachfully.

Rudyard Kipling feels wounded. After all, everyone wants to do his part in the war. Why should his only son be barred from serving king and country? How can they pass over the son of Rudyard Kipling, the most celebrated writer of his time, a Nobel Prize winner?! They can't do that, can they?

In the following weeks, the lines in front of the recruiting offices grow visibly. Every able-bodied man reports for duty, not only in England but in Wales, Scotland, Ireland, Canada, South Africa, India, Australia, and New Zealand. Young men are rising up to fight in every corner of King George's empire. Many of these boys are still in their teens. This is the chance of a lifetime! It is the Great Picnic, an opportunity to see another part of the world. Therefore it's best to sign up quickly, for it will all be over by Christmas. Everywhere you go you see the Secretary of War, Lord Kitchener, on posters with his finger pointing: "I want YOU! Be there! Join your country's army!"

Daddo knows that his pen is a mighty weapon, and he knows that the most powerful people in the land know it, too. He believes that the world must be saved from "the Hun," the name that everyone calls Germany these days. The British world-empire can't just throw in the towel to the enemy!

"Have you read this, John? Fantastic!" Oscar Hornung

says as he flies into Bateman's and takes his brooding friend into the garden.

"What is it?" asks John as he listlessly takes Oscar's newspaper clipping and unfolds it. It is from the *Times*. It is dated September 2, 1914.

"A poem by your pa! And *what* a poem, John!" Oscar grabs the piece of paper and begins to read with gusto:

> *There is but one task for all,*
> *One life for each to give.*
> *What stands if freedom fall?*
> *Who dies if England live?*

The poem, "For All We Have and Are," strikes a chord throughout England. Daddo expresses exactly what the population is feeling. His verses pour oil on the fire and, quick as lightning, they take on a life of their own. The people quickly learn to recite the poem by heart.

A few days later, the great Kipling totally commits himself to the fight. Even though he hates public appearances in which he is the center of attention, it is now or never, he thinks. He rattles off that poem twice in a fiery speech in the southern seaside resort city of Brighton, where he addresses an enthusiastic crowd of young people and urges them to report for duty.

■ ■ ■

"Roberts! Here, look, one of the Irish Guards."

John awakens suddenly with a cry of pain, which sounds more like a hearty burp to the soldier next to him. He is lying on his side, with his torn neck to the sun. His shattered face is glued to a dark-red, sticky pulp on the ground, a mixture of blood, vomit, lime, and clay.

"Please finish me off," John murmurs, but the soldier doesn't understand a word.

The splinters of John's lower jaw pierce his palate and throat. He wants to fight off the pain but he can't. He feels as if his head were being crushed in a vise.

Ma! Mummy . . . Can't anyone help me? Why not? Why me? Oh, God, he complains to himself in disbelief. He slips in and out of consciousness; the battle noises keep waking him.

"Hey, Roberts! Here, I say!" the voice calls impatiently.

Roberts? Which Roberts? Is that old Bobs here? Wait.

Someone is sitting on my shoulders. Now there are two people here.

"Irish Guards. A second lieutenant."

"That's what I said, Roberts."

Oh no, bunglers, amateurs! Just let me lie on my side. Why aren't they helping me?

"Good Lord, Roberts! Look at his face! What a mess."

Lord Roberts? Good old Bobs? Irish Guards, of course. Is it you?

John loses consciousness again.

"Fantastic news, old boy!"

John sees that his father is walking toward him at a pace that is brisker than usual.

"This is for you, Lieu-ten-ant Kipling. Congratulations!" Cheerfully, Daddo waves the letter that his old friend Lord Roberts has just given him in London.

John snatches the paper from his father's hand. "The Irish Guards? Has that good Bobs fixed it up for me?"

Colonel Roberts is an aged veteran who earned his stripes during the Boer War in South Africa. Too old now to be at the army top, Bobs nevertheless has always had his own regiment, and he doesn't want to miss this war.

Daddo isn't totally satisfied. In the newspaper not too long ago he vented his wrath against the Irish, who want to free themselves from English rule. That *his* son must now be thrown together with those Irish! But Bobs is prepared to take John on as an officer, to return a favor; years before, the colonel had asked Rudyard to write for a new army paper, and Rudyard had obliged.

"If you don't think this regiment is suitable for John, I can certainly have him put on a list for a different one," Bobs assures him. But, of course, Rudyard can't dismiss the colonel's gesture. Besides, the list of candidates who are waiting impatiently for their commissions is getting longer by the day. And with John's eyes . . .

The official letter comes two days later, on September 13, 1914. John is appointed second lieutenant, backdated to August 16. Right away he receives four weeks of service time as a gift. The governess and the other servants hurriedly pack Master Kipling's luggage. The next day the whole family travels to London to visit the barber and John's tailor, who works a full hour taking measurements for his uniform. Everyone thinks it's exciting that John's life has been turned upside down in just one day. The Kiplings lunch together in the city and wave goodbye to John at the Warley Barracks, the dilapidated soldiers' quarters in Brentwood, where his regiment has been crammed while training for the fight.

Bad news arrives three days later. After a terrible battle, George Cecil is missing at the front. "Missing in action," Mummy writes. Now John can understand why she was so quiet and anxious when she said goodbye to him. George Cecil, such a splendid fellow—how can that be? George used to visit them regularly. In August he was among the first British troops to be sent to the Belgian front via the French port of Boulogne. The British Expeditionary Force, known commonly as the BEF, has a clear goal: "To stop the German barbarians and save poor little Belgium." Everyone is quite worked up over the graphic stories in the English papers. To their bewildered readers they dish out so-called reports about German atrocities: villages burned to the ground, rapes. Sketch artists show Belgian children being speared on German bayonets, with a devil-like Prussian in a pointed helmet dragging women and girls in the background. The war propaganda machine is going at full speed. Every able-bodied British male should be flying into the action. The papers brush over the fact that in the meantime the inexperienced BEF is being ground into mincemeat near Mons. They are losing almost as many men as the Belgian troops. On September 1, the Grenadiers, young George Cecil's battalion, were bayoneted to death while retreating. John Manners, who was George's best school friend and whom the Kiplings also knew, is dead, that is certain. But George's body has not been found. The strong ties between the Kiplings and George's parents become even stronger. At Bateman's, Rudyard and Carrie sympathize greatly with Lord and Lady Cecil, who are desperately searching for news about their son. The war has suddenly taken on a face. George and his friends are the first who will never return. And the list of dearly beloved sons of friends is growing longer every day.

The tip of my shoe, John thinks when he tries to rub the dried blood from his eyes. *The chalk pit, France, yes . . . First my leg, the German machine-gun nest, the run through the brush, the ear-splitting bang, creeping forward, my head feeling like a block of ice, blood everywhere, terrible, surging pain. Where is the pain? No pain, no, please!*

The chalky field by the Bois Hugo is covered with dark spots from shell explosions, the rims colored red from bleeding bodies. John lies powerless on his side and focuses on that one foot, the tip of his low black army shoe. He is covered in white dust.

"They will shine like a mirror!"

It is so quiet at Warley Barracks that you can hear the wind blowing through the rose beds. The drill sergeant steps past the row of officer candidates and peers at them, boys still, standing stiffly at attention. Only the creak of leather from his coal-black shoes on the concrete pierces through the menacing silence now and then. He turns on his heel and stops by John Kipling. Since John is the smallest, he is standing at the front of the line.

"Isn't that so, *Mister* Kipling?"

"Yes, *sir!*" John says, and swallows.

"Like a mirror!"

John is familiar with military drills from his days at Wellington School. Still, this sergeant-major isn't easy. He has at most a few weeks to take these budding officers, these schoolboys, and mold them into obedient lieutenants who will soon be commanding their own men.

The modern khaki uniforms are inspected: green puttees wound tightly around the calves from the knee to the ankle; the pistol belt at the middle of the coat, with two leather bands rising straight over the shoulders. The sergeant-major inspects each detail. John feels the sweat streaming down his face and neck. The officer lets his eye fall on the flat knapsack. Is the thick winter coat securely tucked away? And who lashed his woolen blanket over his pack like a crushed sausage? He zigzags among the recruits and here and there taps his stick on a hip bag or a bayonet in its sheath. John puffs under his thirty kilos of equipment. Even the ten cartridge holders are full of ammunition; they are contained in five leather pouches mounted on the left and right straps, under the breast pocket. Slung over his shoulder is a rifle, heavy as lead and as tall as John himself.

Just give me a revolver, John thinks. If he could get his gold star, he would gladly exchange this long Enfield for an officer's pistol.

And that gold star comes very quickly. The war won't wait and it is consuming many officers. On the very day

John receives his star, he is standing in front of a platoon of new boys and shouting himself hoarse. John is being drilled on how to drill under the watchful eye of an aging sergeant.

"I'm losing my voice," John writes home, "and my feet are swollen and pinched in those new shoes, but otherwise a soldier's life is wonderful! Sorry, an *officer's* life! For today we've gotten our gold stars."

"That star will be celebrated appropriately," Daddo writes back on the day he receives John's letter. He promises to buy his son a car.

"A Singer?" John's roommates ask in surprise.

"Not a sewing machine, an automobile," John explains. He nods and passes the letter from one bed to the other.

"I honestly don't think that there is a better car to buy," writes his father, the car fanatic. "She is unbelievably strong and fast, and handles so well. And she's terribly attractive."

John's friends are amused as he reads Daddo's letter aloud while stretched out on his bed.

"Of course that little car must have a name," the old Kipling goes on.

John continues: "It must be a famous singer, Patti or Caruso or perhaps Depeche Melba!"

"Car-Uso? Yes, that's a singer. A *real* Singer!" Everyone laughs.

The letter is passed from hand to hand.

"Next week we're scooting over to the city to the theater or the Music Hall!" John croaks in his worn-out voice. Three candidates are sought!" He jumps on top of his iron bed. "Who's going to London with me?"

Chaos breaks out and a list is quickly drawn up.

A few days later the Kiplings pull up in front of the barracks gate. John's sister, Elsie, is at the wheel of John's gleaming Singer, with Daddo seated beside her. Mummy and the chauffeur follow in the *Green Goblin*. It is a happy reunion, with Colonel Bobs, too. John has a pass for that evening. After the mandatory tour of Warley Barracks, during which Mummy continually asks how her poor boy can stand living without any comforts in such a decrepit shack, the flashy party departs in two cars for Brown's Hotel in London. Shortly before midnight, just before his pass runs out, John tears into Brentwood in his Singer.

■   ■   ■

A howling shell skims over the bushes and explodes, carving the sky into a thousand gray, smoking pieces. For one second all is still; then the battlefield is again full of the rattling of machine guns and the cracking of rifle shots.

"We can't leave him here, just look at him."

"He'll never make it, man. He took a direct hit," calls a voice without emotion.

"If this fellow survives, he'll get a one-way ticket home."

A penetrating hiss that drowns out the rifle salvos turns into a raucous whistling sound; it is difficult to determine where it is coming from.

"Look out!" calls a third voice somewhat farther away. "That's for us!"

John can only shut his eyes. A rumbling shakes the earth up under his back. Three seconds later a rolling wave of warm dirt mixed with stinking gunpowder smoke rains down on him.

Home, yes, home! John prays. He no longer tries to talk. A burning pain creeps into his face, mouth, and neck. He clenches his fists and stamps his good leg in utter despair.

Home, Mummy!

Everything is spinning before his eyes.

I'm . . . I'm falling . . . I'm falling . . . No, don't die! Not now, not yet, no! Hold me back!

"Finally, young man. Welcome home!" Carrie Kipling says as she falls into her son's arms. He pulls off his leather racing helmet and goggles and throws them into the open Singer.

"Hi, sis," John says and gives Elsie a quick kiss. "Could you put this machine in the garage?"

Elsie jumps over the car door and drives away in a graceful curve. She takes a short spin through the winding streets, between the tall hedges, and uphill to the center of Burwash. She chugs past the back of the garden ten minutes later. John and Mummy are chatting by the hearth.

"You've changed, my boy. You seem much older." Mummy pulls John out of the easy chair and inspects him. "You're a real officer and gentleman in that uniform."

John beams. He shakes the dust from his coat and examines himself in the mirror. Noticing his mother's worried look in the reflection, he turns around.

"Alas, still no news of George Cecil," Mummy says, reading John's thoughts. She sighs. "Rudyard is doing what he can. He even visited the area near the battlefield at Mons."

"I know," says John. He adjusts his green tie. "Information is scanty for us, too."

"Poor Lady Cecil." She sighs again. "And surely there are many other families that receive no news. Everyone must sacrifice."

John is startled by the number of names she can list. Names with question marks beside them; names of acquaintances, often friends of his and friends of his sister's, too, sons from high society who in these first weeks of war are already missing, badly wounded, or dead.

"Soon I'll have no one to go out with," Elsie cries all of a sudden.

John hadn't noticed that his sister was in the room. She runs up the stairs before he can react.

Mother and son stand by helplessly. Mummy looks outside. John sets his pince-nez firmly on his nose and shrugs his narrow shoulders. Then he breaks the awkward silence. "So Daddo is reporting for the newspaper?"

"Unfortunately. He would have wanted to see you very much. But who knows? He is not far away this time. He's visiting training camps in Larkhill, Bournemouth, and Salisbury Plain."

"You mean our overseas troops who have just arrived." John knows about it from Daddo's letters.

Mummy nods. "You know him," she says, laughing. "Chatting with Canadians, South Africans, and especially Indians. He'll feel right at home. A big child, that's your Daddo."

"Was he terribly shocked by Belgium?" John asks, remembering what his father wrote him about those wounded at Mons. He visited them in the English field hospitals.

"More than he cares to admit." She sighs.

"With a bit of luck I'll be heading into it by the end of the year, Mummy," he says. He blinks. "France!"

But John remains in England. He celebrates Christmas of 1914 with his family at the Aitkens' home in Leatherhead, not far from his barracks. Despite his enthusiasm, his military training has been more difficult than he thought it would be. The harsh outdoor life during the raw winter months undermines his health. And the spartan regime inside the barracks puts too great a strain on his frail constitution. He works himself to the bone, and though his superiors are full of praise, he won't be sent to the front for the time being. "Patience, Lieutenant," he hears constantly. "You're still so young." But John is afraid that everything will be over before he gets a chance to fight. In mid-January 1915, he is overcome by fatigue and stress. He is so exhausted that he has to go home for a little while. His mother spoils him like a baby. She doesn't mention another word about the growing list of acquaintances who are missing in action. Friends and sons of friends who seemed to be adolescents just a year ago are now at their final resting places somewhere in Flanders or France.

John enjoys the rest and the luxury of home. He doesn't even object to Mummy's reading to him when he lies in bed or on the sofa, just as she used to do. Fashion magazines such as *Tatler*, the satirical *Punch*, sometimes a book. *Sherlock Holmes* is nice. *Strange,* John thinks, *that my father's stories also give me a good feeling again. All those years when everyone jeered at me, gave me names from animal stories, grilled me about Daddo – they were either jealous or nosy. Oh, those books! And yet, now that I'm home, all washed out, that one little piece from Father's* Jungle Book *constantly comes to mind:*

> Mowgli laid his head down on Bagheera's back
> and slept so deeply that he never waked when
> he was put down in the home-cave.

■ ■ ■

"Officers aren't exactly poor sods, I tell you."

"Certainly not this one. Just look, what a fine chain."

"Let me see. Hmmm. It's silver, don't you think?"

Why are they fumbling with my coat? John wonders, dazed. *Is the attack over? It's so quiet. There are a couple of shots in the distance. Pain, terrible pain. Who are those men there? Help me. Don't leave me behind!*

John can't turn his blood-soaked head. Black shadows pass through his narrow field of vision in front of the low-lying sun. The silhouettes talk in subdued voices and act as though he isn't there. A quick hand unbuttons his breast pocket.

"Bingo! What a splendid pocket watch!"

"A Hunter. That's worth a fortune. With that chain—"

"'J.K.' is on the back. And it's still ticking. Exactly six o'clock."

From far away a church clock chimes imperturbably through the short, deafening silence.

Six o'clock . . . The words reverberate through John's empty head and carry him four months back in time, from northern France to the south of England, from the front to the army barracks.

"Six o'clock. Dismissed!"

The recruits scatter about the courtyard. Five minutes later John and his friends from the Irish Guards are driving to London in the open Singer. They tear through the street and disappear in a cloud of blue smoke and dust. It is the end of May 1915 and John is on standby for the front. The time has finally come; it's just a matter of days. That's what he hopes, at least. But since he regularly gets a night pass, he and his mates take the car to the city and stay out until the wee hours of the morning.

"Easy does it, young man," his mother admonished him in April, when once again he was sent home for two weeks, completely exhausted.

"That's my boy!" Daddo writes to his son after John describes his nightly escapades at the trendy Savoy Hotel and other pricey nightclubs. When he and Ma think about their frail boy, they are reminded that "in the army you become a man." Daddo believes that no diversion is too expensive for his only son. And perhaps later on he won't be able to indulge him at all, although the elder Kipling doesn't talk about that. Every risk at the front has been thoroughly banished from his thoughts. He laughs heartily at the nightly hell-raising in Car-Uso, which John and his friends bring back to the dreary army barracks by dawn. "That's my boy!" the great writer thinks, delighted. His little boy is becoming a man. And a man must do what is expected of him, certainly in wartime. *Pro patria, pro rege,* for king and country.

■ ■ ■

Damn, those cowards are going to undress me completely. God! Help me! All I can do is move my one leg and my hand a little. Come here, you pathetic grave robbers, you filthy swine, I'll kick you anywhere I can!

"This lieutenant's an angry little bugger, eh, Matt?"

"Surely he's having convulsions?"

I haven't given up, just wait, you idiots. Get your hands out of my pockets! Owww! Don't move me, you bastards, the pain is killing me! If I could just get my revolver. Oh Mummy, help me!

"That wallet isn't up to much, Dick."

Crap! I'll put a bullet through your heads, you scum! And then I'll shoot myself. Mummy! Let me go. I'm going to throw up, I can feel it, no . . .

"Hey Matt, you've got to see this!"

"Give it here. Ah, a photo taken in the snow. This little chap must be rolling in money. Expensive ski holidays with friends, well, well—"

"While we were slaving away in that stinking factory."

Holiday? Snow? Oh yes, Engelberg. Daddo, my dear Daddo! And look, Oscar, good old Oscar Hornung.

Second Lieutenant J. Kipling
Mr. and Mrs. R. Kipling, Bateman's
Burwash (Sussex)

5 August 1915
Warley Barracks, Brentwood (Essex)

Dearest Mummy and Daddo,

What terrible news about Oscar Hornung! The Essex Regiment has lost one of its best men in Ypres. And I have lost my best childhood friend. I can't get his voice out of my head. I can see him in Switzerland, on skis just as always, how we larked about like mad in the snow! I can't believe it. Another of the old brigade is gone. Perhaps he is just wounded or taken prisoner? Poor, dear Oscar.

As for me, everything is going well. The only thing that has taken a lot out of me is the endless waiting for the real thing. It will be a year next month that I stepped foot in here.

It's going less well for our First Battalion. The heavy losses at the front give me a torn feeling. So many friends will never be coming back. But at the same time that increases my chance for receiving marching orders to France.

Lieutenant Colonel Edmond (the Earl of Kerry), who has command of our battalion, assures me that he is satisfied with me and that August 17 is written in his appointment book. Then I'll be eighteen! Kerry (that's what the men call him) says that there will be nothing more to hold me back. I'll let you know as quickly as possible if there's big news!

Big fat kisses (for you too, Elsie!),

John

P.S. Sorry, Daddo, I'm afraid that Car-Uso *has had a little accident. Perhaps we'll have to scrap him. (It's rather serious. I'll explain later.)*

P.S. 2 Before I had a chance to mail this letter I heard the shocking news about Julian and Bobby Grenfell. Our friends, Lord and Lady Desborough, are being sorely tried: two sons killed in six weeks' time. Now they just have Yvo. He wants to begin his training after Christmas, when he's seventeen. It's a meager comfort for Julian and his parents that he had family at his bedside in Boulogne when he died. (Kerry says that Monica, Julian's sister, is a nurse at a field hospital in Wimereux, near Boulogne.) This is probably not news to you. Kerry showed me Julian's poem, "Into Battle." It appeared next to his obituary in the Times. *A posthumous rival for Daddo. (Why didn't anyone tell me about Bobby and Julian before now, anyway?)*

▪ ▪ ▪

Second Lieutenant John Kipling is known to be a very reasonable officer among the regular recruits. Of course he is also the son of a living legend, the wealthy writer whose stories and poems are taught in all schools. But John tries to forget his background when he's with the officers. They appreciate the modesty of their youngest colleague. In the officers' mess John is the cheerful, humorous lad with the tiny little glasses, a hard worker who is always ready if his lieutenant-colonel calls for a volunteer.

But outside the barracks John changes back into a rich kid, a posh boy, an expensive dandy. When he is out at night, either alone or with friends, and parks his Singer (which has been repaired) in front of an extravagant hotel or a swinging concert hall, he enjoys having the porters, bellboys, waiters, and butlers in livery, waiting on him before he even walks through the door. He spends more on tips than he earns as a lieutenant.

"I've gotten a bargain," he writes home. "For barely three pounds I've signed up for a temporary wartime membership to the Royal Automobile Club."

John doesn't say a word about the truly royal amounts he spends in the plush salons of his club. *That's my boy!* Rudyard thinks once again. Englishmen's clubs, and certainly those in London, provide an atmosphere that will turn his boy into a genuine English gentleman. *And an automobile club to boot!* cheers the car-crazy Rudyard to himself.

Father and son meet for the last time on August 11, 1915. John is spending the night at the Bath Club, Dover Street, London. Rudyard is spending the night there, too. In no time at all the private club fills with members who "by chance have to be in the area." Nobel Prize winner Rudyard Kipling is a star, and the members practically fight over the tables to get a glimpse of him. It is he, not John, who will be going to the front the next day. *The Daily Telegraph* has asked him to write a series of articles entitled "France at War." Since Rudyard couldn't have a military career himself, he is glad to be right there in the action to report on it. He believes that the war is a heroic fight against the barbarians, and that the noblest fate a young man could encounter would be to give his life for his country. He recalls the words of Horace,

"*Dulce et decorum est pro patria mori,* How sweet and honorable it is to die for the fatherland." As long as it's not *your* son . . .

Two days later the Irish Guards Regiment in Warley Barracks receives an important visitor: Lord Kitchener, the Secretary of War. He has come to inspect John's battalion and solemnly inaugurate it. It is now no longer a reserve unit.

John goes home for the last time that evening, on August 13. He brings along his friend, Rupert Grayson, who stays just an hour at Bateman's. The heartfelt farewells to Mummy, Elsie, and the trusty household staff are postponed until the middle of the night. Rudyard is in France. "Send my love to Daddo." Those are John's parting words as he stands at the top of the stairs and wishes his mother a goodnight. His unit leaves the barracks in Brentwood on August 15. The next day he makes the trip across the English Channel between Southampton and Le Havre. John finally lands in France on August 17. It is his eighteenth birthday.

■ ■ ■

John often sailed into the harbor at Le Havre on his way to Switzerland. He now feels the same marvelous thrill as he did when he was ten, at the side of either his governess, Miss Ponton, or his father. With his nose reaching just above the railing, he would be full of anticipation as he watched the gulls, the approaching coast, the ocean liners with their smoking funnels, and the bustle during docking time. This is his first birthday without his family. Eighteen! He doesn't miss them, however, for his men are standing right behind him. They are waiting just as impatiently as he for the Great Picnic.

"It's going to be fun, Rupert," John whispers to his friend, who has come up on deck for a while. "Finally *la douce France!*"

"Wine and women, eh, John?"

"Ah, *oui, mon cher, du vin rouge!*" John answers in impeccable French. He sighs.

Rupert tries to speak French, too, but his tongue is tied up in knots: "*Ah! Lay de-mwa-zelles wro-man-ti-ques*! Girls, eh, old chap!"

The boys are relieved that they have made it to France in time; after all, everything will be over soon. They are sure of it.

It takes an eternity before their ship, the SS *Viper*, docks. Hundreds of fresh troops, grouped in dozens of platoons, stand on deck and watch the cables grind against the steel mooring posts. While waiting for one of the heavily laden platoons to move, Lieutenant John Kipling, apparently relaxed, follows the tense actions of the sailors on board and the dockworkers on shore. Short, sharp whistles send mysterious commands to the navy personnel. Three gangplanks are set down. John is sitting with his men on the quay ten minutes later. They laugh, they smoke, but mainly they wait. John exchanges a few words with the sergeants, then gathers together with the other officers.

There is an extra-wide gangplank mounted on the SS *Viper's* bottom deck. A small tractor uses it to pull dozens of fully loaded horse carts from the stern onto the wharf. The horses, with hoods over their heads, come separately. Led by their attendants, they clatter down the iron plank one by one. Stubborn or nervous animals are led back to the nose of the ship, where a crane is lifting the loose cargo out of the hold. Carts are being transported, too, and they swing on long hooks as they are moved over the railing to the quay. The horses come next, and what follows is a spectacle that the amused people down below have never seen before. The officers and their men watch as the helpless, bawling animals, suspended on long straps under their bellies, hover over the water before they are plumped down on the dock. The teamsters curse to each other and plead with the panic-stricken beasts to help make this unusual task manageable. A fiery, dark-brown racehorse lands too hard on the concrete and falls to its knees. Hundreds of "Ooohs!" from the shocked spectators reverberate over the wharf, as well as hundreds of boos directed at the crane operator. A shot rings out five minutes later. The animal has been put down. The men are quiet for a moment. The carcass is dragged away by one of the work horses.

"Lieutenant Kipling?"

"Yes?" John says and looks around, surprised. A corporal from the military police salutes and hands him a letter.

"For you, sir."

It is a telegram from Daddo, wishing John luck on his eighteenth birthday:

AM IN VERDUN ON ASSIGNMENT—STOP—WAS HOP-
ING TO MEET YOU ON THE BIG DAY—STOP—CAN
ONLY SEE YOU IN LE HAVRE AS I PASS THROUGH—
STOP—SPENDING THE NIGHT ISN'T ALLOWED—
STOP—MAYBE JUST AS WELL ON YOUR BIG DAY—
STOP—PERHAPS WE'LL MEET LATER AT THE
FRONT—STOP—LOVE DADDO—STOP—

John answers him the next day. He sends the letter
home because Daddo has no other permanent address.

*I am writing this in a train proceeding to the firing
line at 15 miles per hour. We are due at our destination at 11 a.m. tomorrow. I am quite concerned about
my men, for they are all sitting on top of each other:
the whole battalion of 1,100 men are jammed together in one train, along with 73 horses and 50 wagons.*

*Three friendly (and pretty!) English ladies pam-
pered us with coffee and tea and large slabs of bread
and butter during one of the countless stops. They
run a stall just like the ones you frequently see in the
French stations.*

The adrenaline is visibly rushing through the veins of the subalterns. They can feel the danger approaching. For the time being they have great fun polishing off bread, sardines, and jam, and washing it all down with whiskey and water. They stick their bare feet out the window and sing and shout and smoke like Turks while waving to the startled passersby. It's quite all right here! This is A-1!

Would you be so good as to send me an Orilux service lamp for officers? Don't forget the refills. I'm enclosing a newspaper clipping; the French press keeps a close watch on Daddo.

The Second Battalion of the Irish Guards disembark at Lumbres. From there the troops march for days over the endless *pavés,* the brick roads, toward the front. Field officers proceed on horseback. Young officers such as John Kipling and Rupert Grayson walk next to or in front of their platoons. "On our God-given two legs!" Rupert says with a laugh.

At night they fall exhausted onto their straw mattresses.

"I'll strangle that miserable shoemaker for ramming these nail heads into my soles," John complains.

It remains hot and dry. The steel-blue sky shimmers and the severity of each day's march is measured by the merciless pull of their shoulder straps. After half a day, a rucksack weighing thirty kilos will feel as though it weighs a hundred. At least John and Rupert don't have to lug their leaden packs and heavy rifles, for the officers' baggage is transported by horses and mules, together with the munitions and tents.

For the time being, the endless *pavés* are their greatest enemy, certainly for the ordinary infantryman and the petty officer. Each extra mile is measured off with uncertainty. John can't let on to the fact that he, too, is taking his bearings through the clouds of dust that follow the regiment over the landscape, and that he is unsure of the landmarks on his map.

"Acquin," he said to his platoon. "That's the destination."

"All right," Sergeant Cochrane conceded, after he was shown how the route had been mapped out on paper. That boosted the men's spirits.

John wasn't really surprised when Cochrane walked up to him hours later.

"With permission, sir," the sergeant said hesitantly. He did not look happy.

"Sergeant?"

"Of course I don't want to question the decision of an officer, sir, but are you certain that—is this the correct way?"

"Happy that you mentioned it, Cochrane."

"The boys, sir. Uh, not ours. Well, I mean the men in the platoon behind us. They say that we've taken a wrong turn."

John takes his map and pretends to study it. "Then is this the road to Lauwerdal, and not Acquin? Or no—"

"Le Poovre," the sergeant says, correcting him. He looks straight ahead. "It was marked on a washed-out little arrow sign on a wall, they say."

"Just now?"

"An hour ago, sir."

The difference in rank between officer and sergeant is great, not to mention the difference between officer and ordinary infantryman. The stiff etiquette of the English army makes that gap unbridgeable. But the young Kipling, with his brand-new gold star, must gather all his tact and courage to inform the regiment commander of the mistake. The long procession is stopped. Picnic, they call it. Scouts on horseback head out immediately.

A rocket shoots into the sky half an hour later. The Irish Guards continue on in the same direction for two miles, then take a right turn off the cobbled road. Making their way on bone-dry church paths and farmers' roads, they curve back around toward Acquin. This way it seems no one has erred and no one suffers loss of face, certainly not the officer who plotted out the route. It is even amusing as they goose-step between the grain and flax fields. The boys are able to try out their French in a field where women and men are binding the harvested flax into endless rows of knee-high sheaves to dry. The farm girls don't understand a word of the soldiers' exuberant French, but that doesn't matter; a smile is enough to drive the boys crazy.

Young pups like John and Rupert can be quite sympathetic to most soldiers in spite of the military etiquette. The junior officers, after each exhausting day's march, must make sure that their men find suitable shelter, negotiate with the local citizens if necessary, see that rations are evenly divided, and take care that the feet of their troops are inspected and patched up. Only then can they pass the command to the noncommissioned officers and find beds for themselves.

The marching is hard on everyone in the Guards even after the rigorous training at Warley. They march up to forty kilometers a day with full packs. The young officers such as John and Rupert have great admiration for Captain Harold Alexander, their company commander, for he marches every mile with his men. "It's the same distance on foot as it is on horseback," he explains, dead serious. Alex would later be promoted to field marshal and "Duke of Tunis." He had been wounded in November 1914 at Zillebeke, near Ypres. "Oh, that little scratch," was his invariable comment about it. That attitude alone is enough to grant him a good deal of authority and respect among the men. His unbelievably sharp sense of humor, which is in such startling contrast to the stiffness of "the real Englishman," makes him hugely popular. Alex keeps the morale of his troops high. He promises the worn-out boys a surprise on one of those hot, wretched, dusty days. That evening the whole battalion sits exhausted on the ground around an improvised stage, amid bottles of beer and illegal French wine. Alex appears on stage wearing a crazy hat that goes quite well with his enormous mustache. The unexpected sound of accordion music turns all heads to the scene. In a few seconds the long, nasal wailing creates the same excitement as a drum roll does before a death-defying leap. Alex stands still and as stiff as a board. An accomplished Irish dancer, he begins to hop back and forth to the simple, monotonous chords of the accordian, with his upper body taut and his arms pressed to his sides. The whole crowd springs up in madness. The handclapping of the Irish Guards swells to a rhythmic ovation. Alex lets himself be whipped up by the foot-stamping and the Gaelic yells of his men, and in an instant they all forget about their fatigue.

John and Rupert also try to get through those difficult days by singing their misery away. Their fired-up marching songs acquire a few new racy lines each day.

> *Here's to the Kaiser, the son of a bitch,*
> *May his balls drop off with the seven-year itch,*
> *May his arse be pounded with a lump of leather*
> *Till his arsehole can whistle "Britannia for Ever."*

John is discreet in his letters home and doesn't write about this part of the musical repertoire.

"Oh, Rudyard will most likely find out about them,"

says Rupert. He is amused to see his friend lie on his bedding and fill up whole sheets of paper with his scribbling.

"I can't tell my father about things like that," John answers. He is well aware that Mummy will also be reading every word he writes. He also knows she shows off the letters to her chic circle of friends, women who probably all have a hero in the family.

"At home they'll be eager to read the *franglais*," John adds.

Rupert chuckles in agreement. "Frenglish!"

The British soldiers speak a roguish kind of French and call out all sorts of things to the girls along the way. It provides some comic relief each day.

"Talking French they are screamingly funny," John writes to his family on August 20 from the small but comfortable village of Acquin, near Saint-Omer.

We are splendidly billeted here. There are about fifty men in every barn in the area. I myself have accommodations in the mayor's house, where his very attractive daughter lives, too. Monsieur le maire *is a small-time farmer but he reads. He stood up to wel-*

come me as his guest, the son of "le grand Rudyard."
His daughter's name is Marcelle, Celle to her friends.
It will be good for my French. . .

As a member of the upper class, John has always been able to speak the language of Molière reasonably well. Daddo reads effortlessly between the lines and knows how smitten his dear son is. Head over heels in love, or even more. Perhaps a romance is blossoming. Daddo writes back, "The best dictionary for French is a dictionary in skirts."

John always receives a lot of letters from home; every day in the barracks at Brentwood, every four days in France, for the mail can't be delivered more often than that. Mummy and Daddo don't miss a day. And in addition to letters, they send him countless parcels. "John Kipling!" the courier calls when he empties his mail sack. "Lieutenant Kipling! For you!" John is buried under the wool pullovers, collars, underwear, and stockings that his overanxious mother sends him. And all the while northern France is groaning from the heat, dust, and flies.

"Surely our whole company is wearing something of yours," Rupert Grayson says with a laugh.

The parcels are getting to be an embarrassment. John writes to his mother and begs her:

> *Please, no more underwear or clothes. Send me some biscuits instead. (But not the digestive kind!) Also welcome are chocolate (for the food is rotten!), a refill for my Orilux lamp, Colgate tooth powder, tobacco, shaving powder, magazines, and a glass (in a box for traveling), writing paper (also for my men who can't write; I do it for them) . . .*

Even in Acquin, the Guards barely get any time to sit around when the long day's march is over. There is drilling, shooting practice, hours and miles of marching, then more drilling. The worst marksmen have extra shooting practice.

On August 30 they kick up their heels and take the day off. The Second Battalion of the Irish Guards plans to rendezvous with the First Battalion—their equal—halfway between the two, in Saint-Pierre.

"Unbelievable, isn't it, Rupert? Just think: they fought at Festubert, Neuve-Chapelle, and last year they were even in Ypres!" John is practically floating when he thinks about meeting the First Battalion.

Rupert remains sober. "Don't forget Mons. That was last year, too."

"Oh, that was the beginning of the war," John says, waving the criticism away.

"Right. But then George Cecil and his best school chum, John Manners, of the Grenadiers, were there as well."

"In God's name, Rupert! What are you trying to say?" John snaps back. No one likes to talk about the British Expeditionary Force, for instead of freeing poor Belgium it was all but wiped out in an instant. This army of professional soldiers was sent to Belgium and northern France at the onset of the war, but it was too small and too inexperienced to stop the Germans.

The encounter with the First Battalion is a shock. The brave and seasoned soldiers don't seem like heroes. Most of them look drained and pitiful. Even their uniforms appear faded and weary; the badges on the sleeve and the glittering harp on the collar are often missing. While they march over the sunlit field by Saint-Pierre, John and the other boys of the Second Battalion watch them silently.

But the new recruits like John Kipling, Rupert Grayson, and their men are so keyed up for battle that they aren't put off. Everyone is impatiently awaiting the real adventure, the confrontation with the barbaric Huns, the exchange of gunfire, and, who knows, perhaps a chance to be a hero. They hang on the words of their colleagues. Powerful stories are savored with a few glasses of "plonk," French white wine, while Captain Alexander sits on a table under the sheltering trees and cheers up the whole crowd with tunes on his harmonica.

Some soldiers in the First Battalion are not cheered up by the festivities.

"Those boys all grew up together," a young captain says with a sigh. He has noticed that John is looking inquisitively at three silent young men who are sitting farther up in the grass and staring straight ahead.

"Oh yes, we have that in a couple of platoons, too," Rupert Grayson interrupts, a bit too cheerfully. "Are they chaps from the same district who reported for duty together?"

The officer nods, frowning.

"Fantastic, isn't it?" John exclaims. "True comrades, together in the fight."

"There were eight boys in that group on Wednesday." The captain presses his lips together.

There are no further questions.

That night, John tosses and turns in bed until very late. He sees his fallen friends George Cecil and John Manners standing beside him. "With waxen, freshly washed faces that were smiling at me," he will tell Rupert Grayson much later. "Their uniforms were full of bullet holes and bayonet cuts, and blood was everywhere."

John breaks out in a cold sweat in the middle of the night. Shivering, he takes some writing paper. He sees the glazed eyes the Irish veterans of the First Battalion marching back and forth in his head looking like porcelain dolls. "Some look like animated corpses," the young Kipling will later write home. "Real walking corpses, so exhausted and knocked about. From the beginning they've gone through an unbelievable number of battles—often with heavy losses. We're still brand-new to this."

■ ■ ■

Mummy? Is that you, Ma? Yes, that does me good, rubbing my forehead like that. I can't open my eyes very well, Mums. Wait. Ow, that hurts. Careful with my head, oooh. Steady with my neck. That's better, rub there a bit. My eyelashes are stuck together.

It is late in the afternoon on Monday, September 27, 1915, on the battlefield of Loos. The road that rises gently from La Bassée to Lens cuts the grand French-Flemish fields down the middle. The chalk pits are on the right, just past the hamlet of Hulluch. A little farther along is the village of Loos, with its church in the center. Next to the main road is the Bois Hugo, a forest on a hill. Between the road and the forest lies a wounded boy in a disheveled uniform. A gold-colored harp is sewn on his collar, but in the sinking afternoon sun this emblem of the Irish Guards is covered with blood. Lieutenant John Kipling opens his eyes with difficulty. He is awakening from a brief coma. Disoriented, he slowly regains his senses. He can barely move and he cannot speak.

"There you are, sir. You have lost a lot of blood," he hears a deep, friendly voice say.

Who is that, John wonders in a daze. *Where am I? A cap, the army—France, the front, the attack.*

The day's events come to mind like a festering sore that breaks open suddenly. At the same time a searing pain jumps from his leg up to his head. His body is racked with spasms.

"Quiet, sir. Don't move," the man says. His voice is soothing. His silhouette blacks out the low sunlight as he bends over him. John's gaze now falls on the man's white armband and a dim red cross upon it.

Could it really be bad? Oh, my face is burning. Dear God, man! Keep your white rags away from my face! Nooo, that fellow is stripping the skin off my head. Stop! Make him stop!

The army medic sees the pain and panic in John's eyes and the taut muscles in his legs. "Quiet, Lieutenant. I've got to stop the bleeding. You've lost too much blood already."

John tries to cry out but his vocal chords are gone. His faltering breath is barely audible and becomes lost in the pink air bubbles and brown froth that well up from his formless mouth and ravaged throat. *Don't let me die, please take me with you*, he begs with his eyes. He looks back and forth and follows each move of the medic with suspicion.

"Shhh. Above all else don't move, sir. We'll take care of you. Quiet now, please." The man drops his arms to his side and shakes his head.

John faints, but a voice rouses him instantly.

"We'll never be able to bring this one back," the medic calls out to someone nearby. "Impossible."

John listens intently. There are gunshots as always, in the distance. Men are groaning not far from him, voices that beg for help. *What are they calling out? Do I know that voice? Or not? My platoon—how are they doing? Have they made it?* Shells and grenades skim by overhead. There is cursing from the medics. *Is that why they don't dare move me? The ground is shaking a little underneath me. There, now I hear missiles exploding in the distance.*

A second army cap turns and floats above John's face.

"Goodness gracious, no." A man with a higher voice speaks close to his ear. He sighs. "It's best for this one to stay here. We'll lay him a bit farther up, in a ditch."

"The nearest trench is on that side," says the man with the low voice. "At least he'll have a chance there. The poor devil will be hit with more shrapnel if we leave him here."

They're afraid, John thinks. *They're going to let me die here.* He feels like a boxer who has fallen in the ring, knocked out by a double uppercut, down for the count. He closes his eyes and hears the din swell all around him.

The two medics begin to argue. They pay no attention to John, for they believe he is unconscious.

Hurry up, you amateurs! John rages to himself.

"They're fast approaching now," calls the first medic. "Come on, man, grab his feet."

"Leave him, there's no point."

"Come on, man, this is an officer. We can't just ignore him."

"Officer, my arse," shouts the other.

The low voice becomes raised. "To the trench with him, I tell you! Quick, before it's too late!"

"And we'll put a gas mask on him, too," answers the second medic cynically.

John is becoming nauseated from their bickering. And from the pain. He tries to think about something else. *Trenches, gas masks . . .* The words reverberate through his head.

■　■　■

"My God!" John shouts. He has been blasted awake by a sharp bang and by his own loud voice. The straw mattress slips off his bed. For a second he thinks they are being attacked by German artillery. But that's impossible, he realizes, because the Fritzes are too far away. A long, drawn-out crack from a nearby bolt of lightning fills the small guest room. John gazes suspiciously at the beam above his head. *Boom!* Light flashes through the curtain just before a second clap of thunder shakes the room. Only now is he aware of the rain that is beating down on the tiled roof.

It's the first day of September 1915, John thinks, and he swings his legs out of bed. The season is changing and the rain will be welcome indeed, for it will cool the air and wash away the dust and the flies.

"Holy cow! Damn!" His feet are in a puddle on the floor. He is surprised by how quickly he has picked up the swear words of his men. Water is trickling along one of the edges of the roof and down the wall behind his head. He mops the water around his bed and grabs the white enameled chamber pot from the cupboard. "I can't fill it up this morning, anyway," John says to him-self with a chuckle. He sets the pot down against the wall behind the bed.

John is free this morning. Because there is no inspec-tion or morning exercises or drill, he can take his time breakfasting with his host family. When Celle, the daughter, moves her chair and cutlery closer to him, he pretends not to notice. She sits right across from him, beaming.

"Quel temps, n'est-ce pas?" John begins.

Her father, who is sitting next to John, growls some-thing like *"oh-la-la"* and looks worriedly outside.

John continues to talk about the weather so the man doesn't pay attention to his blushing daughter, who is rubbing her leg against John's. She has kept her eyes on him all week. Yesterday she launched the attack for real. While milking the cow in the little stall, she called to him as he walked by.

"Is it true what they say about *les Boches,* about what the Germans do to women and children?" she asked. She kicked the door shut behind her, cornering him to prevent an escape.

John can still feel her whispering breath in his ear. "Of

course it's true," he answered hoarsely. "Otherwise I wouldn't be fighting here. Those dirty Huns drag innocent women away by the hair after they've speared the babies on their bayonets."

"Innocent?" she said. There was something strange and confusing in her voice. *"Vraiment innocentes?"* It was so cramped in that tiny space. She kept moving closer. He pushed his glasses a bit higher up on his nose.

Innocentes? John had seen it with his own eyes, certainly on posters about "poor little Belgium" which stated, "Their women are being murdered, or worse." And the newspapers had reported it, too. The *Daily Telegraph* was regularly sending Daddo to Belgium and France, for that matter.

John had never been so close to a girl's face before. When someone began to fiddle with the door handle, his lenses fogged up. Even the cow was jumpy, and Celle rushed back to her milking stool. Later on he could not remember what he had said to her mother as they each sidled through the narrow doorway.

And here she is again, sitting right across the table. Actually it's exciting to be so near to Celle.

"Oh-la-la, quel temps!" The kitchen door swings open

and her mother staggers inside, dripping wet. "It's a strange sight, all those soldiers with their brown capes in the rain. *Les pauvres.*"

"I've got to go," John says, and he jumps up. "Breakfast was delicious, *merci.*"

He walks along the Rue de l'Eglise with his head down and his hands deep in the pockets of his leather raincoat. It is difficult to see out of his thick glasses in the pouring rain. Dozens of soldiers are walking around the little marketplace. Water is streaming down the rain capes that they wear over their shoulders. *They look like shiny dancing bells,* John thinks. John hurries up the steps of the parsonage, where their temporary headquarters have been established.

"Ah, Lieutenant Kipling!" Captain Alexander says. He is in a cheerful mood. "The new gas masks are here."

"That is good news, sir, although I don't think we should be expecting a gas attack in this weather."

"Kipling, Colonel Butler wants *you* to be in charge of training the men to use the new masks."

"Well, thank you, Captain." John swallows.

"Thank *him,* old boy," Alex replies, giving John a poke in the ribs. "I think the colonel is right. It's just as well to put those new things in the hands of young officers. Go ahead, test them yourself. You're free this morning, aren't you?"

The captain points through the window to the motorized wagon in the courtyard. "Those ten crates there. Twelve dozen gas masks in each one."

It has been rumored for weeks that the British and French troops are about ready to try their hand at using poison gas. John doesn't even think to tell the captain about this state of affairs. The battalion commander himself has not been informed about his army's new top-secret weapons.

For a long time the horror of chlorine gas was the No.1 topic of conversation at Warley Barracks and at John's London club. At the end of April 1915, the newspapers were positively drooling over this lurid subject. "Our boys" put up considerable resistance in the Second Battle of Ypres, they wrote. From a maze of trenches, the British and French had been able to hold the front line that curved around the city of Ypres, but it had cost thousands of lives and many appalling injuries: men whose eyes were burned out, whose lungs had burst. Even the best soldiers were powerless against those surprising gas attacks. The bizarre frontline command, "Piss on your handkerchief! Hold it over your mouth!" was thought to be rather amusing back home in England. "But what else could we have done? Nothing, God damn it!" Nigel Francis said bitterly. He was an officer stationed at the front but was home on leave one month after the attack at Ypres. John had met him by chance quite some time ago, during an evening out in London, just before Francis was sent to the trenches in Flanders. Lieutenant Francis was a quiet, amiable student. When John ran into him again in May, he almost went right past him, for Francis looked like a sick, older version of himself.

"You would—oh, God!" the young man exclaimed. "You would have gone mad if you had seen those poor boys spitting their bleeding lungs up. Hundreds of them all at the same time. It was hell! Their eyes and throats were on fire. That's why all those who could still get away jumped into the water. The canal by Boezinge was full of dead bodies." John can still picture Nigel Francis biting down on his knuckles as he finished his story.

John also recalls hearing about the African soldiers who were suffocated during the gas attack. They were dressed in gaudy red trousers and fezzes. They had just arrived in Ypres from the French colony of Senegal. "How scared those wogs must have been!" everyone in the gentlemen's club exclaimed, and they laughed. They felt worse about the two thousand Canadians who were defending Ypres. Their task was to close a five-kilometer-wide breach, and they died near Saint Julien while doing so. Strong stories, all, which John and his friends usually enjoyed with a crystal glass of whiskey and soda as they lounged in the club's plush easy chairs. He remembers how he and his mates tried to outdo one another with their knowledge of the deadliest gas formulas and powerful poisons. They felt like true military gentlemen, a little club of merciless warlords.

John knows that at the firing lines the fear of gas and the elusive enemy has been firmly instilled. And now that his battalion is moving closer to the front, he can feel a change in the atmosphere, too. When they were at Brentwood, they practiced using those first gas masks until they were blue in the face. The "smoke helmets" are awful for John and other boys who wear glasses. Thick, smelly canvas caps is what they actually are, and treated with chemicals that cut off your breath. There is a little pipe for blowing out air, and two glass peepholes that break almost of their own accord. Pure misery.

John Kipling spends the whole afternoon hauling chests of gas masks. He recruits about ten men from his platoon to help, for an officer is there to give orders, after all. The boys are relieved to be inside in such nasty weather. The ten crates are unloaded in a shed by the parsonage. With united effort, the men then drag the crates one at a time onto the empty veranda and break them open.

The new gas masks look exactly like the old ones, and stink just like them, too. "They have the stench of a corpse," John remembers his drill sergeant at Brentwood saying.

They've delivered the wrong ones, John thinks for a moment until he unfolds one. This model has flaps over the glass, he notices to his relief.

"Gas!" he shouts half an hour later. "Attention! Smoke helmets on!"

They are practicing in a greenhouse used for growing grapes. *It's a nice place for a drill,* he muses; there is plenty of light, it is cozy and dry, and his voice sounds the same as it does outside.

"In God's name, Johnson, those eye flaps must be shut. That's precisely what they're for."

"Yes, sir."

"Break just one piece of glass and you'll be mopping all the floors of the parsonage!"

The flaps appear to be working. The drilling with gas masks is a matter of discipline. Flaps are shut when folding them up; flaps are opened when the thick linen caps go on the head. The men practice putting on the masks over and over again, until they can take them out, put them on, fold them up, and put them away with their eyes closed. And along with those masks, they have to cope with those military caps, always a major production.

"Hup! And one, two!"

Ten masks are raised into the air. *They look ridiculous,* John thinks, but this is a matter of life and death.

"Flaps off! Now! One, two!"

The soldiers practice putting on the masks while lying down, standing up, and while running in the courtyard between rainstorms. One after another they begin to gag from lack of oxygen within the airtight linen mask.

"Sergeant Cochrane, can you take over for me for a bit? Fifteen-minute break. Be especially careful that the masks are fully closed under their coat collars."

The sergeant salutes briskly. "Yes! Sir!" he replies, satisfied. At least *he* doesn't have to put on that suffocating cap anymore.

The officers have a pleasant time together that evening. John demonstrates his drill technique on his lieutenant colonels. He bites and barks out orders to them, for that is what they want him to do. But they laugh and drink together, as well.

"Gas, gasss," cries someone who comes bursting into the room. "Help! Smoke!" Thick clouds of smoke pour out from under his cap.

Quickly they remove the mask to reveal Captain Alexander, armed with a fat cigar.

"They call these things *smoke helmets*, don't they?" he says, and he roars with laughter. "That smoke is worse than I thought!"

The Irish Guards have difficult days ahead. The officers are more aware of this than ever. The daily marches now run about twenty miles, and there are military maneuvers on the program, too. It's tough luck, for the heavy rains continue. But above all, a command to march directly to the front could come any day.

One night, John and Rupert are a bit tipsy as they walk back to their billeting quarters.

"You have nice lodgings, don't you?" Rupert teases.

"They're all right," says John.

"Et les femmes, mon cher? Celle is her name, isn't it?"

"Who says?"

"The walls have ears, Kipling!"

Actually Rupert has no idea about Celle's aggressive moves. But John can't resist telling him about his adventure in the cow stall. Rupert is green with jealousy.

"Hey, man, let's trade places. It's dark, at any rate, and she won't even notice."

"Not for love or money!"

They chase each other down the street like two schoolboys.

"See you tomorrow!" Rupert calls, when John closes the garden gate behind him. "And give her mother my regards!"

John chuckles and walks past the dimly lit kitchen window. In the darkness he can't see a thing. By groping he finds the stepladder to the attic above the little barn.

Five minutes later he opens his ink pot and begins to scratch his pen across the paper.

■　■　■

Second Lieutenant J. Kipling
Mr. and Mrs. R. Kipling, Bateman's, Burwash
(Sussex)

2 September 1915, France

Dearest Mummy and Daddo,
We are still in the same village, far enough from the front, therefore safe. Not allowed to give names. Understandable. The people I've been staying with have been very kind to me.

Tomorrow we're moving to X for the Brigade Field Days. Long marches, actual war drills, fighting techniques, making trenches, evacuations. We'll be sleeping there. This is real. I'm looking forward to it. However, it's raining just as hard and long as it does at home. English weather.

That leather jacket is as heavy as lead, completely soaked. On the field I'll have to use those clumsy army canvases. For that matter, the mud is also a problem during the street marches. Wait until we're lying in our trench.

Will you send me the following items right away:
a genuine navy oilskin, pipe cleaners, a tin box of
matches, and some dry underwear.

The oil lamp on John's table begins to flicker all of a sudden. A draft comes through the floorboards. He lays down his pen. The rustle of trees rises up the stairwell. Has the door blown open?

"Is anyone there?"

No answer. The rustling stops. He hears only the water dripping off his raincoat onto the wooden floor. He holds his breath for a few seconds. There is silence.

John picks up his pen again and tries to read the page, but a tread creaks on the steps. And another . . .

■ ■ ■

Two brown eyes stare at John, motionless. They look right through him. He lies bleeding in a ditch. This is his very first field battle. He is slipping in and out of consciousness. And he is waiting, helpless.

John glides forward on a cottony little cloud through

a milk-white haze and lands soundlessly in the grassy ditch. Slowly he awakens once again. A shadowy form is beginning to appear above his face. Everything he looks at is barely visible without his glasses. His myopic gaze zooms in on two glassy eyes that are wide open.

John squeezes his own eyes shut. He has a terrifying thought: *It's the Angel of Death who has come for me!*

The motionless face hangs over the edge of the ditch, a half-meter from his very soul.

Is this the end? John thinks. *So fast? Don't look at me like that! Jesus, I can't move, I can't even turn my head away.*

Blood oozes from the dead man's ear. The drops roll over the grass and are immediately absorbed into the pink, chalky soil.

Could that be me? Am I already dead? Is it a bad dream, an image of myself? Say something, you creep! Why is this Grim Reaper so quiet? God, what's happening to me? I can't talk, my mouth doesn't work. And that horrible fellow doesn't say a word either! He won't budge. Everything is spinning around me, everything is black . . .

■ ■ ■

I'm living, I'm still breathing. Where was I? Oh, that wretched man. He's still lying there. His eyes. Go away! I can't do anything for him. Hmm, look at that, his arm. There is a white band on his sleeve, a red cross. That's the medic who wanted to help me. He's dead. That can't be, can it? Two—there were two of them. Could the other one be dead, too?

Listen! Someone is calling for help. Voices. Someone is crying. Why don't I feel anything? I can't feel a thing! Maybe it's better this way, without pain.

Listen! The road. Army cars are driving past. Ambulances, perhaps. Can they see me? No, they keep going. Patience, have patience, they will come. Above all else I've got to stay awake, I mustn't die.

There they are again. Engines chugging, autos are riding past me. Did I fall asleep, after all? Stay awake, think, fight, that's what I must do. Those cars. Think about home. What's it like in Burwash now, at Bateman's, our house? I wrote to them just last week about cars and such. Maybe they're reading my letters right now.

Dear Mummy, Daddo, and Elsie. Or should I say Phipps these days? Yes, Elsie, I hear from Daddo that

you have a new nickname. By the way, how is my
car? I wish I were a fly in East Sussex, dear sister, so
I could watch you parade around in my Singer.
Daddo writes that you already can handle it rather
well. Is it true that he is considering leaving the
Green Goblin in the garage for the rest of the war?
You've become his permanent chauffeur, he says.
Those Singers have proven to be useful in France, too.
At the Divisional Headquarters I've seen two and
they're exactly like my Car-Uso. I've got to restrain
myself from getting in one of them and tearing off with
it. If I'm lucky enough to survive this adventure . . .

*Did I really write that? "Survive?" God, no! Don't let me
die. I knew that this might end badly, but I didn't think I
would die. No, not that! They will find me here, won't
they? I don't want to die. They can't just leave me here,
can they? No, someone will come looking for me soon.
I've got to control myself. Calm down, Kipling. Quiet,
you're not an officer for nothing. Oh, I feel so tired and
empty, I want to sleep. No, old chap, pull yourself
together. Wellington School, drill, discipline, Brentwood,
Warley—keep at it. Don't sail away now, stay awake,*

you've got to think. Those letters. Think for a moment. What else did you write?

If I'm lucky enough to survive this adventure I'm going to get myself the smartest two-seater Hispano-Suiza that can be bought. What a splendid car it is! And what a sharp engine it has under that graceful hood! But what I want more than anything else when I get back is a nice hot bath. You people at home can't even begin to realize what excessive luxury surrounds you. We're killing ourselves with endless marching and I've had quite enough of it, with all the dust and the bugs. And when it's not boiling hot, the rain pours down incessantly. We're fighting against the mud, lice, and rats. Those rough Irish boys in our regiment can withstand this abominable outdoor life better than we boys from wealthy English families. What I'd like first and foremost when I come home is . . .

I'm so tired. I want to sleep. Miss Ponton? Will you bring me upstairs? My bed.

■ ■ ■

A motionless figure is lying in a ditch. An inexperienced English officer. He is a small detail on the battlefield at Loos that Monday, September 27, 1915. The British front-line pushes a kilometer farther to the east. The Irish Guards and the Scots Guards gain some ground on this day, just barely crossing the road that rises gently from La Bassée to Lens. The Germans are still defending the area. John is lying near the road, right by Pit 14, a lime-stone quarry between Chalk Pit Wood and the Bois Hugo. They are strange words, marks of identification, really, like Lone Tree in the same vicinity. These are the last words that Kipling read; they were notated on his military map.

English with some French in between, John muses. *When I was a child we mixed the languages together and called it* Franglais. *Daddo and I used that jargon when we wanted to be secretive. And my friend Oscar. Poor Oscar. "Je believe this vraiment est le grand jour, mon friend." Elsie would find it a nice mélange, Oscar too, and Daddo.*

The low, dull droning of a machine gun startles John out of his dozing thoughts. He listens intently. *The*

artillery sounds far away, deep in the woods. Such a poor, endless rumbling can't possibly be directed at one precise target.

He tries to concentrate on the pumping noise of the artillery. That's all he can do, but it helps him forget the pain that is welling up again.

Damned Germans, he thinks, *they're firing blindly in order to give cover to their men who are advancing. They're trying to win back territory. Shhh. Jesus, oooh, my face. Mummy, help! I can't take it anymore. I'd rather shove my head in a bucket of boiling water. Oh, God! No!*

His whole body shakes. John can't cry out, for all that remains of his mouth, nose, and throat are some holes and patches of raw flesh. With his one hand he reaches for his head, but he lacks the coordination to do so. Exhausted, he drops his hand to his side. The shaking increases until once again his body is racked with spasms. Then, as if by magic, all movement ceases. John lies there and waits. For what? For whom?

Fifteen minutes have passed. Or is it five? He doesn't know. *Rifle and pistol shots.* John awakens in a daze. *The pain is gone again. The pistol shots sound harmless and almost ridiculous compared to the heavy machine-gun*

rounds. A counterattack with little toy cap guns, but it keeps getting closer. A shot is fired back every now and then, a cracking sound from the other direction followed immediately by an echo from the quarry.

A thumping noise now, footsteps and stamping on the ground close to his ear. Dim, hurried shadows dart past the corner of John's eye. He can't turn, and from his ditch he sees only the gray-blue sky, the sparse red tops of a few trees, and two brown, hollow eyes in the questioning face of the dead medic.

Someone is panting close by. There is a rustling of leaves.

"Guck mahl hier, ein Offizier!" a voice mutters in surprise.

Two hands reach out for the shoulders of the dead medic, who has been hanging close to John's face all this time. John sees the bloodied head give a brief nod — *Like a quick greeting, a wink, see you later!* — after which the corpse is rolled away, disappearing with a thud into the grass next to him.

"Herr Hauptmann, hier legt ein Leutnant!" the same man calls to his superior, who has caught up to him.

God, Fritzes are all around me. John weeps silently,

helplessly. Tears of pain, rage, and disillusionment roll down the remains of his tattered cheeks.

Three men in mouse-gray uniforms gather around and by turns bend over him. One man kneels down beside John.

"Mein Gott, dieser Kerl lebt noch!" My God, this man is still alive.

A hand waves a black Luger pistol above him. The man mumbles something in unintelligible German and searches all of John's pockets.

What are they looking for? They won't find anything on me. Ugly Hun, I won't tell you anything, ever, do you hear? John is seized with a painful cramp in his chest. Coughing and choking, he spatters blood all around. The German jumps back, cursing.

The pain ebbs quickly and John feels a strange laugh coming on. *I can't betray anything at all,* he realizes, *even if I wanted to. How can I talk? You've shot me to pieces.* For a moment it's a crazy, restful thought.

Now what? They're beginning to turn me over. What are they looking for? They're getting snappy, they're at the end of their patience. Oh, just listen to them bark at each other. I wish they wouldn't keep waving their weapons around. This will come to a bad end. Mowgli! Mowgli, help me! The Bandar-log *have nabbed me!*

The men stop their bickering and are quiet, all of a sudden.

How is it possible? John reproaches himself. *I hope no one finds out that I panicked! Be strong, fellow. Remember your rank. Even the enemy must treat an officer with respect. That was the agreement, wasn't it?* he thinks nervously. *Listen up now, or I'll call Mowgli!*

John could have done without that little boy from his past. Mowgli, the "man-cub" who was raised by wolves, was the hero of his father's *The Jungle Book*.

Once, John now realizes, *Mowgli also fell into the clutches of the enemy, the Monkey-People, the* Bandar-log. *Mowgli — God, how I cursed that little chap. I've never felt any kinship with that jungle brat. But when there are Germans pointing guns at your head, that changes the picture; you start having second thoughts about it all.*

When John was a schoolboy he was always being compared to the man-cub from the jungle, even though he tried to avoid it. There was absolutely nothing wild or exotic about him, with his pince-nez and skinny body.

He *did* enjoy some of his father's stories, but he hated *The Jungle Book* like the plague. Mowgli had been pursuing him since childhood, always and everywhere, even when he first joined the army. And now Mowgli suddenly pops up on his own accord.

"Hey, Kipling!"

John sees himself as a ten-year-old again, a beanpole at Saint Aubyns Prep School in Rottingdean.

"Look at him there, Mowgli the Frog!" Fingers point at him.

"Afraid of the big bad wolf, man-thing?"

Those same troublemakers practically fell over when they heard that this slender little four-eyed kid, this young Master Kipling, was not a bit afraid of the dark. They learned about this after the night when John stole out of the dormitory to drive away evil spirits for his friend Beresford. Ever since that night he could count on being given a little credit, at least.

"It's a shame that I'm not good at sports," John daydreams. "My eyes, you see, these nearsighted eyes. Although you know, Daddo, no one can beat me at swimming."

"Ha ha! Of course. Swimming isn't difficult for a frog!"

"Yes, they keep on teasing me, Daddo. I'll just have to get used to it. And why do you find it so necessary to torture me with your famous books and poems? I've often written to you about it. When *Puck* appeared, naturally the schoolmasters knew to fish out that instructive closing poem, 'The Children's Song.' Every single day at school all of England, no, what am I saying, the whole British Empire sings the song written by the great Rudyard Kipling. I sing it, too. Certainly I sing it, for the schoolmasters make very sure that I do. 'Kipling this, Kipling that.' I just *hate* it! And then there is 'If,' another big hit. Every single boarding school has the verses of 'If' hanging on the wall, either painted, framed, or engraved. For punishment we have to write it out until our fingers are numb. Why do you do this to me, Daddo?"

Hey, don't touch me! What does that fellow want from me? Ow, that hurts! If you want to empty my pockets, you're too late, you fool. They've already run off with everything. Though I don't know what they could have stolen. Some pounds, at most?

"Hauptmann, hier, eine Karte!" comes a voice.

My map! That bastard has found my map! Filthy Fritz!

The three German soldiers now turn their hurried attention to the document, ignoring the small British lieutenant lying motionless, waiting to die. They crowd together above him; the German captain snatches the map from the hands of one of the other soldiers and unfolds it right over John.

My map! John could kick himself. *Good Lord, what's marked on it? Our positions? Names of army units? Notes? What doesn't a person put on such a scrap of paper?*

"You can't be too careful with military documents and notations at the front, you must guard every single piece of paper." John can still hear his instructors call out those words. They drilled it into him countless times. Even the most inexperienced officer knows these strict orders. From underneath the unfolded paper John hears the three Germans deep in discussion. He thinks back to the middle of September, two weeks earlier, when it had become increasingly clear to his battalion that their first attack was drawing near.

■ ■ ■

"Come on, Rupert! Bring that chap down! Get him!" John is shouting at the top of his lungs.

"Shoot! Now! Shoot, I say!" Voices from the other side are shouting, too.

"Get him, Grayson! No. Rupert! Ohhh, too late!"

Cheering comes from all the soldiers on the sidelines. They are amused at the sight of the players, all officers dressed in short pants revealing their white bowlegs.

"You aren't a footballer yourself, are you, Kipling?"

"Uh, no, Colonel." John is caught off guard by the unexpected appearance of the corps' commanding officer, Lieutenant Colonel Butler. "The football is a bit too round for my two left feet," he quips, trying to save face. "Water sports, sir. I'm better at them." Clumsily he hops from one foot to the other.

The old aristocrat takes his time, twirling the tip of his mustache with his thumb and middle finger. "I see. Rowing, eh, Lieutenant? Or sailing."

"Swimming, actually, sir," John says and waves his arms, pretending to do the breaststroke. An unnecessary gesture, absolutely ridiculous, he realizes.

"By the way, Kipling. Mister Grayson is your friend, I assume."

"Rupert Grayson is a very good friend indeed, Colonel."

"And the soldiers in our battalion, as well?"

"Indeed. Well, uh, of course not personally, sir." His glasses begin to slide off his sweaty nose. He pushes them back up. "They're not personal friends."

"I should certainly hope *not*, Kipling. If your father were to hear of it! Don't forget that they're Irish. And *you*, after all, are an Englishman."

"Well, sir, I didn't mean . . . "

Colonel Butler is not listening. John snaps to attention.

"*We* are officers, is that what you mean, Kipling? And *they* are our subordinates."

John stands somewhat ill at ease and looks at the improvised football field. The colonel is directly next to him, gazing out over the field while he talks. The referee sets the ball down in the middle and blows his whistle for the new kickoff.

"Of course, Colonel." John's easygoing manner has completely taken on the strict, submissive tone of the military.

"And your friend, *Mister* Grayson. Is he an officer, too?"

"Of course, sir. He is a second lieutenant, the same as I." What a question! John thinks. The colonel taps his wooden officer's stick against his riding boot.

"Precisely, Kipling," says the colonel. "Look here, good fellow, even though we're off duty, I would appreciate it if you would no longer address Grayson as 'Rupert' in the presence of subordinates."

John swallows hard. "Naturally, sir. It won't happen again." He pinches the side seam of his trouser leg.

Colonel Butler walks to the end of the football field, which is lined with the caps, shirts, and jackets of the players. John flashes a look of relief to his fellow officers. They can barely contain their snickering. The colonel then turns around unexpectedly.

"Oh yes, Kipling. You've just been promoted to two-star lieutenant, but of course we'll wait for the official announcement."

John stands ramrod straight. "Thank you, sir," is all he can manage to say.

His promotion is not unusual. The officers at the front are put through the meat grinder so fast that they are constantly being replaced. One very quickly becomes an *ancien* in a fighting unit.

"Congratulations, old chap!" a sweaty Rupert Grayson says and pats John on the back after the game. "That old battle-ax has laid down the law, I hear."

"Oh, yes, *Mister* Grayson!"

The other young officers burst out laughing.

"A fine football match, Rupert," John continues, "but think about your fans, and shave your legs in the future!"

"Hear, hear!" The gentlemen surrounding John shout their approval.

A fight begins seconds later. As the two friends roll in the grass, the other officers gather round and cheer them on. As if by magic a swarm of soldiers, corporals, and sergeants flock to the scene.

"Look out, *Second* Lieutenant Grayson," jokes Captain Alexander, who has pushed through the pack. Lieutenant Kipling is now your superior!"

"I'll show *him* some stars, more than he can pin on his uniform," Grayson shouts.

The duel turns into a true farce, a grotesque cockfight. John and Rupert put on a show, the audience quickly take sides, but in the end John is pinned on his back amid a cacophony of boos and cheers.

"What will you do for me?" asks a sneering Grayson.

"Fine, fine, *you* win!" John calls breathlessly. "I'll buy you a drink."

Rupert Grayson looks doubtfully at the crowd as he holds down his friend. He knows that the young Kipling is rolling in money.

"Is that enough, boys?"

"No!" they shout in unison.

"And also a drink for the men, a drink for everybody!" John says desperately.

Rupert lets him go.

Alex jumps into the circle and takes each fighter by the hand like an official referee. "And the winner is…" To the surprise of everyone, he raises John's arm up high.

The soldiers laugh, they boo, they whistle and yell, they push and pull one other. New fights break out here and there, and caps and coats go flying into the air. The whole battalion is keyed up.

"Our men really needed this," Alex says into John's ear. "They needed to let off some steam." He turns to Rupert and says, "Thanks, boys."

During the past days all the soldiers and junior officers alike have been asking themselves just how far you can push military drilling. Conditions for the Brigade Field Days had to replicate actual life at the front in every respect. The men practiced their new fight techniques endlessly with and against other regiments, as though their very lives depended on it. They dug ditches and trenches, rolled out barbed wire, crawled through mud, lay in waiting for hours at a time, exposed to all the elements, sometimes in the pouring rain. The weather was unpredictable and always seemed to be against them. They were hustled out of bed for nightly reconnaissance patrols. They scraped together their last ounce of strength for hand-to-hand combat, carrying heavy packs and wearing gas masks as they did so. It never stopped. Their nerves were dangerously on edge. They staged mock attacks using real smoke shells. John's battalion even captured a real village for practice and interrogated French citizens, escorted prisoners, slaughtered pigs, and sought shelter for the night. They knew how critical their situation was, and fear was building up inside everyone. The moment of truth was approaching. The next day or the next week they would have the real enemy in view.

"A bullet in the leg," Rupert proposed to John one

evening. "That wouldn't be a problem."

"Or in the arm." John thought that was reasonable, too. "Maybe a couple of fingers gone, although . . . " He noticed that Rupert unconsciously put his right hand under his left armpit.

"Have *you* been worried about it lately, as well?" Rupert asked hesitantly. He could sense John's fright by his silence and by the expression in his eyes.

Fear was taboo. This was the first time the two friends dared to talk about it.

"I'm beginning to realize that I may never see England again," Rupert confessed.

"The best-case scenario would be a gunshot wound, or a bit of gas," John said, thinking aloud.

"Dear God, not in the belly," Rupert mumbled. "Or my face. I always think about that. Or a bayonet wound. Yikes!"

"I don't want to be crippled. Be completely dependent on others. No, not that," said John with a sigh. "Or blind."

"How about a bullet to the shoulder?"

"That would be acceptable."

. . .

The football matches on that Sunday, September 12, 1915, were well-timed, a welcome change. The men desperately needed something to ease their stress. First the soldiers and corporals kicked the ball around together. Then came the long-awaited spectacle of the officers in their shorts. Those stiff English gentlemen could finally appear in a different role, and the Irish Guards would talk about it for a long time afterward.

The football games appeared to be just a warm-up. The staff officers had prepared well for this day off. The field kitchens stocked special provisions for the occasion, including meat, vegetables, and tinned fruit. There was a barrel of rum for each platoon, and the quartermasters distributed chewing and smoking tobacco. Here and there an accordion or Irish flute was hauled out. The vast field was teeming with exuberant boys. They laughed and shouted, drank and smoked. A concert in the open air began after nightfall. Enormous torches were set around the podium. The entertainers wore the same uniforms as the audience. They were professional musicians and actors who traveled across the entire front in Belgium and France, from one regiment to another. They knew exactly how to handle this rough crowd. Those who shouted the loudest were chosen to come up and dance, and their antics were such a farce that their comrades were soon rolling on the grass with laughter. But it was just as easy for the musicians to silence the men, and at the first notes of "Oh Danny Boy" the audience fell completely quiet. The song sent chills down each spine:

> *Oh Danny boy, the pipes, the pipes are calling*
> *From glen to glen, and down the mountainside.*
> *The summer's gone, and all the roses falling,*
> *'Tis you, 'tis you must go, and I must bide.*

> *If you come back and all the flowers are dying,*
> *And if I am dead, as dead I may well be*
> *You'll come and find the place where I am lying*
> *And kneel and say an "Ave" there for me.*

With a lump in the throat the Irish boys sang the refrain in harmony. Here and there a silent tear glistened in the flickering light. Those tears were quickly wiped away, for the next medley of songs made fun of the Germans. The excitement built, and the musicians gave it their all in the last encore.

The day concluded with a huge campfire. Once again the men sang from the very depths of their souls. They drank, too, for then they didn't have to talk. Or worry. No one said a word about what would be happening in the days to come, but everyone was thinking about it.

The officers drank another round just before midnight. Finally they could talk freely among themselves.

"That wrestling match this afternoon was splendid!" Alex said to John and Rupert. "Cheers, Kipling. To your health, for that matter!"

"Will you let your family know about your promotion?" Rupert asked John.

"It will have to appear in the *London Gazette* first," said the captain in a kindly voice. "You know that, don't you, boys?"

"I'll wait," John declared. "I wonder when they'll find out for themselves."

∎ ∎ ∎

"We are on the eve of the biggest battle in the history of the world!" Lieutenant General Haking solemnly proclaims three days later. It is September 15, 1915. The commander of the Second Guard Brigade is never shy about speaking to his assembled officers in a self-important manner.

"The time has come!" John mutters to Rupert excitedly. Feelings of relief and high expectations fill the general staff's big tent. Friends nod to one another.

Most of the men have not yet been to the front. They are very proud indeed that a general is taking the trouble to speak to even the youngest officers of the whole brigade. John becomes quiet when the commander–in–chief hands out his specific commands.

"Everyone will strictly adhere to my orders. Think about your training, follow the instructions. Trust your superiors. On Friday and Saturday we'll do one last test: field practice together with an artillery division and the military engineers. Tomorrow we'll march to Wisques. It's close by, to the south of Saint-Omer. Gentlemen, the hour of truth is near!"

The general speaks in a melodramatic tone, but John is completely taken in. *Is that so?* he wonders.

"Don't leave anything to chance," the general continues. "The enemy mustn't get a single break. Be especially careful with military documents at the front."

John feels as though he is floating. He thinks about his sister and the carefree days when they rowed together on the narrow Dudwell River, which winds through their country estate. The water mill way in the back of the lush garden, the perfect hideout for boys like him. His motorcycle. His mother. And Daddo, of course. They would be so proud of him now!

Lieutenant General Haking's nasal voice brings John back to reality. The commander–in–chief raises a glass with his most important staff officers and ends his speech in a stately manner. "Gentlemen, your country is counting on you. To victory!"

The crowd applauds politely. Glasses clink together.

"To the king!" Solemnly, the general sips his champagne.

"To the king!" the men call out in unison.

When the speech is over, the junior officers of the First Battalion are hardly impressed by the general's words. Quite the contrary.

"The general is a real strategist," says someone scornfully. "Unbelievable, isn't it, so much experience."

"Yes, with little tin soldiers," answers another. "His house is full of them."

"The general just wants to see his name in the news-papers."

"In the want ads," a third officer jeers. "Brains wanted. Apply to the Second Guard Brigade!"

They chuckle and smirk, but on each face is a bitter smile. John can't understand why these sarcastic remarks are being made behind the general's back by officers in the First Battalion, of all people! *They* have had experience at the firing line, haven't they? And it's precisely *those* men who seem to have no interest what-soever in Haking's words!

"Captain Alexander, you were wounded at Ypres," John says, completely confused. "How can *they* make fun of . . ." He can scarcely find words to express his indignation.

"They've described the general exactly," Alex replies, trying to quiet him. "Look, whoever returns from hell only *half* shot to smithereens considers himself lucky."

"Hasn't the lieutenant general served at the front line himself?" Rupert asks.

John looks wordlessly from the one to the other.

Alex shrugs his shoulders and sighs. "If you survive a battle, the first thing you do is count your fingers and toes. *If* they're still there. Then you count your comrades on those fingers. After each attack. And each time you'll have more fingers left than friends."

"And in the long run only your fingers remain," a voice calls out bitterly.

The three turn around in surprise. They see a young captain from the First Guards, a tall, round-shouldered fellow.

"And all your comrades—gone in a flash. Gone forever." His dull, black-rimmed eyes look right through John. He taps his cap in salute, a small, emotionless gesture. Then he disappears among the other officers.

"Poor Davis," Alex whispers. "He's lost two brothers. One was just a couple of meters from me. Shrapnel was flying all around. The splintered tree stumps were full of that glowing metal. Davis's youngest brother was bent over, seeking cover. It happened quick as lightning. One moment he was watching me, waiting for a sign to go over the top. I can still see his friendly, confident gaze. A boy who was burning with energy. A second later there he was, blown to pieces. Not a pretty sight."

■ ■ ■

The map is jerked from above John's face. There is a flash of light. The German soldiers look up in alarm. The smashing blow from the mortar shell comes quickly, taking them by surprise. Unable to run for cover, the three are blown away. Although John lies protected in a ditch, for a moment he can feel himself being lifted up in the air. The explosion sucks all the oxygen from his lungs in one fell swoop. He lands hard on his side, unconscious.

Minutes later his eyelashes begin to flutter. From the corner of his eye, John looks in a daze through the blades of grass. He sees a gray cap with gilded piping a couple of steps away. Thinking is painful. The German officer, yes, now he remembers. A contorted body lies a few meters beyond, smashed against a tree. Between the cap and the corpse are the blood-spattered remains of his map. John is suddenly aware of a total silence; he has been completely deafened by the explosion. The pain begins to pound in his brain like a battering ram. Once again blood oozes from his open skull onto the remains of his neck.

Jesus, no! John screams without a mouth, without a

voice. *Oh God! Let me go!* His body twists and shakes. For many minutes.

My head is about to explode. How can I fight off the pain? Swallow, gasp for air, clench a fist. Help me! Isn't there anyone coming this way? Then let me drift away, please! Or die, perhaps?

The pale evening sun reflects off the chalky-white wall of the limestone quarry. The mysterious glow that it casts over Pit 14 is in sharp contrast to the darkening surroundings. The eerily calm trees of the Bois Hugo and Chalk Pit Wood are veiled in the twilight. Silence rules; the void is complete.

John Kipling is quiet now. He draws on the last reserves of his strength. He has never felt so lonely, not even in the dreary dormitory of Saint Aubyns Prep School. He realizes that no one can see him. All hope is lost. As he lies near the pit, he thinks about Celle once again.

"Ne pleures pas, don't cry, *ma petite,"* John whispers. He has had only two minutes to give Celle the bad news, for

her mother is coming around the corner. He wants so very much to comfort the girl.

It is Monday, September 20, 1915. John is spending the whole evening in the company of his host, the mayor of Acquin, and his wife and daughter. His marching orders came this afternoon. Tomorrow they must move up toward the front. Their destination is Linghem, twenty miles to the southeast. Their quarters in the cozy little French village must be evacuated in a hurry. The battalion spent the entire day breaking up camp, packing, and loading up the horse carts.

A carton full of tinned goods has been set on the kitchen table. It is a gift for Celle's family: fish, meat, and fruit, all overstocks that the battalion doesn't want to drag any farther.

Celle's father, an admirer of Rudyard Kipling, is surprised at the sudden departure of the troops. He wants to ask for a favor, and quickly. On the table next to the tins is a pile of Kipling's books in French translation.

"*Mon papa* Mister Kipling is coming to France at the end of the week to report for the newspaper," John says. "To Rheims."

"*Une petite chance* perhaps that he'll come visit Acquin?" asks the mayor, beaming.

"*Ah non, désolé, monsieur.* He knows that I'm moving. But I'm not allowed to tell Daddo where I'm going."

"Daddo?"

"*Son Père, Papa.*" Celle jumps in to help.

"*Ah, bon,*" says the mayor.

During this whole time the girl has been staring at John with a dreamy look in her eyes. The young man can barely keep his mind on the conversation; the mayor must explain everything two or three times.

"*Ah, mon anglais,*" says the good man, who hardly knows the difference between "yes" and "no." "My English is not that great, *excusez-moi, mon lieutenant.*"

"I often think about my *pauvre maman,* now that the big day is approaching," John lies.

"*Naturellement.* I wish that your papa, *monsieur* Rudyard, was here, lieutenant. *Hélas!* But would you be so good as to write something in my books? *Un souvenir.*"

John can forget about having a little time alone with Celle. The mayor tells him his thoughts about each and every book, droning on and on while John inscribes them. It is growing late. Celle's mother stands up.

"The men are sure to have a lot to discuss," she says. "Come, Marcelle."

There is an awkward silence as John and Celle part with a respectable, but very prolonged, handshake. They can barely get the words *"au revoir"* across their lips.

John spends the entire night on the guest bed, staring at the shadows that are dancing in the lantern light. He waits for Celle, but the steps never creak.

■ ■ ■

The march to the southeast to Linghem via Estrée-Blanche is spread out over two days, much to everyone's relief. Yet the company commander has little compassion for his foot soldiers and devises some drills to compensate for the possible time loss. The men have no idea what the front will be like, and they are worried about the events to come. Will I survive the baptism by fire? Will I be wounded? Where? I must be strong. But still, will it be a bullet, or a piece of shrapnel, or chlorine gas? Not a bayonet, please!

In the meantime the senior officers are driving their Irish Guards to the ends of their patience. The young lieutenants are overwhelmed with orders which they must unwillingly impose on their men.

"Horrible, isn't it?" John exclaims, when the exhausted boys are obliged to perform their shooting maneuvers while wearing a suffocating gas mask.

"I'm not going to contradict you," Rupert says grimly. Twice each soldier must creep and crawl around wearing that heavy canvas cap while shooting off a full load of cartridges.

"They won't be in any condition for the *real* fight later," John says to his friend. He sighs.

"Don't show your displeasure. It's bad for your authority."

"*You* should talk, Rupert!"

On the way to the front the troops are provided with more equipment, munitions, and reserve weapons. The junior officers must throw out half their personal belongings, for the horse carts are overloaded.

"*Dear old F—,*" John writes to his family on Thursday, September 23.

> *It made my heart bleed to leave a lot of my splendid*

kit by the wayside. My finest shirts and underclothes,
all my books and magazines, my luxurious toilet kit
and my supply of Colgate and shaving powder. Even
my Orilux lamp. We are quickly approaching the
front line now and will soon be engaged in our first
battle. In the meantime send me a really good pair of
bedroom slippers (with strong soles). And a tooth-
brush. I'll let you know what else I need later on.

Saturday, September 25, 1915, is a busy day. Muster is sounded at five o'clock in the morning. John Kipling and the Second Battalion Irish Guards leave their quarters in Linghem and join the rest of the brigade ten kilometers away, in Auchy-au-Bois.

Field Marshal Douglas Haig is watching the smoke wafting from his cigarette at that same predawn moment. The wind is okay, or nearly, anyway. The commander of the First British Army Corps makes a bold decision, from the safety of his plush headquarters, far behind the firing line. For the first time he orders British soldiers to use the new weapon, poison gas. The command comes five months after the Germans launched *their* first gas attack north of Ypres, which took thousands of British, French, and Africans by complete surprise and caused them to die in a most gruesome manner. Field Marshal Haig hopes that his use of this suffocating gas will force a decisive breakthrough in northern France.

Eighteen-year-old Lieutenant Kipling doesn't know this as he marches in the direction of Loos, between Arras and Ypres. The wind is unpredictable. The main consequence of Haig's decision is that the British will be sowing death and confusion among their own men. Adding to their failure is the fact that the Germans are far too well prepared for a gas attack and will shell many of the British gas cylinders. Furthermore, it will take hours before all those cylinders can be turned on, because someone brought along the wrong keys. It is a series of blunders of monumental proportions. But John doesn't know any of this. He dreams of heroism in the starring role of his life.

At Loos nine hundred boys in the King's Own Scottish Borderers also dream of their part in that great adventure. Encouraged by the squealing of bagpipes, they set foot on the black plain at Loos on Saturday, as well. Doesn't Field Marshal Haig know that they don't stand a chance, for they won't find cover anywhere? Certainly he has heard about the German underground bunkers, hasn't he? Hasn't he examined the aerial reconnaissance photos, the maps with German trenches and barbed wire notated on them? The Scots are like walking targets as he sends them directly toward the safely hidden machine guns of the enemy. Two men of the nine hundred men will survive. For weeks the open field will be strewn with the bodies of the dead men, their kilts flapping in the wind. Corpses will be hanging all along the barbed wire, too. The Scots of the Black Watch won't fare much better: all their officers will be killed, and more than half their men. And to their horror, the next day the British officers will receive the same orders to attack from the superior army command. Of the ten thousand British troops at Loos, over eight thousand will perish, in less than four hours. And not a single German.

But luckily John Kipling will never know any of this. On that rainy Saturday morning he proceeds with the Irish Guards from Auchy-au-Bois to Burbure. In spite of the overwhelming stress of the past days, John enjoys watching the endless rows of soldiers marching in their ranks behind and in front of him. What kind of enemy could ever take on these boys? "The biggest battle of all time." General Haking's words echo in his head. *Great generals can see into the future,* John muses. *Perhaps a page of history will be written here. Julius Caesar must have felt like this, or Hannibal.* John marches proudly next to his platoon. He gives a pat on the shoulder here, an encouraging word there. This is the real stuff. All his weariness has fallen away.

The situation changes at about ten o'clock. The narrow cobblestone roads become clogged with the bustle of men, animals, and army cars. Hundreds of cavalry rush past John. Marching in orderly rows is all but impossible. There is practically no way to get through the villages. Startled horses slip on the wet *pavés*. John's platoon scatters. A young sergeant falls under his mount and breaks a leg. He lies groaning in the gutter while a group of men tries to catch the snorting mare.

The chaos reaches its peak before noon. Military police must direct traffic at the intersections, with red flags and whistles. Whole companies are being turned away from their frontline destinations. Dark figures in grimy uniforms come hobbling in small groups from the side streets; they don't look like the fresh troops at all. They are returning from the trenches for a break.

Usually they are relieved after four days and nights at the front line—if they are still alive. The boys seem as though they are from another world. They have a strange look in their eyes that they try to hide under the dripping-wet visors of their caps. The noise and chaos on the roads doesn't affect them. *Where are their officers,* John wonders. *Don't they have an ounce of respect in the least?* Neighing and shouting resounds on all sides. Carts rattle past. The *clickety-clack* of horseshoes on the paving stones is making the troops crazy. Teamsters curse and brush past the Irish Guards as they drive their skittish horses and stubborn mules toward the front. The route is dotted with manure, stinking garbage, soggy food remnants, and discarded gear. The Irish treat the advancing cavalry to the choicest curse words that their rich Celtic language has to offer.

On the way a courier delivers a telegram from Major General Cavan, who wishes them "God speed" and a "good journey." The nervous boys are now beginning to realize that the great battle has actually begun. What will it look like? The main road becomes even more obstructed by the onrushing vehicles. Ambulances honk as they thread their way through the disorganized crowd. The men are finally getting a taste of the war. The first shocking images pass by scarcely one meter away: farmers' carts stacked with corpses. Sometimes those carts are stalled in traffic. You can touch these bodies; they are real. And they are clad in British uniforms. Rain mixed with blood leaks out of the wagons and runs in red streams onto the cobblestones. The commotion dies down for a little while. Horribly mutilated boys ride in open wagons past the advancing troops, crying fearfully. The spectacle sends shivers down John's wet back. You can actually smell the front now.

Quarter to two. Burbure is an ants' nest. The Irish want to pitch their wet tents in the unprepared village. The officers seek accommodations with the citizens, but army quarters are completely full. Everyone is dead tired. Reproaches fly through the air. The men are pushing and pulling and fighting among themselves. The company receives an order to continue to a couple of villages farther on.

After marching feverishly for fifteen hours, the Second Battalion Irish Guards are absolutely soaked when they reach their temporary shelter. It is one o'clock in the morning. Tents, sheds, barns, huts, empty stalls—anything is good enough to house the more than one thousand soldiers, corporals, noncommissioned officers, the horses and mules, and almost thirty officers. The men bed down amid a great deal of moaning and groaning. John and Rupert then drag themselves to the officers' briefing.

Colonel Butler is formal: when the news comes, everyone must be ready to proceed to the trenches within thirty minutes. The front is less than two hours away by foot. Each company must have two men posted to sound the alert. John finally heads to a farmer's barn and sinks down to the straw, exhausted. It is the middle of the night. He has a splitting headache. He wants to sleep, but he's much too tired.

■ ■ ■

Sleep, headache. Yes, I want to sleep, nothing more . . .

A lean young figure is lying in a ditch next to a woods by the village of Loos. It is Monday, September 27, 1915. The Bois Hugo is a sad, lonely place to die. His officer's tunic is crumpled and covered with mud and lime. It looks like he has two different legs: there is a khaki-colored puttee on one calf and a gleaming red and brown one on the other. The blood-soaked cloth has become loosened, yet it binds the wounded flesh together. A round, dark bloodstain stands out against the sparse grass that surrounds his head. The ring is growing wider by the minute.

Let me sleep and never wake up again, John Kipling prays silently. *This awful pain is keeping me awake. Someone is driving one nail after another into my head. God, it's horrible. A wild dog doesn't deserve to die in the jungle like this, not even Tabaqui, the Jackal. I'm being skinned alive here. Mum! Mummy, how long do I have to keep this up? Mowgli can't stand it anymore, Daddo. Akela, Father, Wise Gray Wolf, take me to the Peace Rock so that I can throw myself into the Wainganga River . . .*

"Twenty-five *Fritzen!*"

John can picture the little stone building by the chalk pit during the first attack a few hours before.

"Good work, Sergeant Cochrane!"

"Dead Germans are good Germans, sir."

"You're wounded, Cochrane."

"That leg of yours looks worse than my shoulder, Lieutenant."

"I've done well, haven't I, Daddo?"

"Sorry, sir?"

"Has that machine-gun nest been put out of action, Sergeant?"

"It's been completely destroyed, sir."

"Do you know my father, Sergeant? This is the great Rudyard Kipling!"

"Hello, Sergeant. How do you do?"

"Excuse me, sir. What do you mean, Lieutenant?"

"I'm going to die, Daddo. Hold my hand tight. Are we going to scout out this building together? Daddo, I'm going to die."

"Come, come, my boy. Who dies if England live?"

"Tell me anyway, Daddo. Tell me I've done well!"

"Of course, boy."

"Daddo, I'm getting my second star soon."

"Aha, that's more like you, John. That's my boy!"

"And that's all there is to my whole life, Daddo? That's it?"

"Yes, boy. Giving your life means you'll live in eternity."

"Just one time in combat? No more than that?"

"*Pro patria, pro rege.* For king and country."

"*One* battle? For *that* you've groomed me and molded me since childhood, Daddo?"

"The king will be satisfied, John. God save the king!"

"Is this really all, Daddo?"

Suddenly two arms reach up from a ditch at the edge of a woods called the Bois Hugo. The thin hands grasp at the air. The arms stiffen now, then fold quietly and come to rest on the little officer's chest and he lies on his back like a fallen saint, with the palms together and fingers and thumbs pointing toward the sky. He is not breathing. His body is seized with a powerful spasm. His arms reach out one last time; it is the image of a diver getting ready for the plunge. John Kipling tumbles into space and disappears into the water of the Wainganga in a slow, graceful curve. A red ring is left behind on the Peace Rock, like a halo.

■ ■ ■

A long, chilling scream pierces the heavy silence behind the dark doors and thick walls of Bateman's. A jolt is passing through the Kiplings' centuries-old house in Burwash. Three separate doors open as the kitchen maid, gardener, and butler come bursting into the parlor with puzzled looks on their faces. Rudyard Kipling is slumped in an easy chair, grasping the armrests and weeping hysterically. He rants and raves like a man fighting with death. His glasses are on the floor. A telegram is crumpled up next to him. The servants stand there, bewildered. What are they to do? They shouldn't be witnessing this, certainly not in the presence of Bonar Law, the leader of the Conservative Party. After the king and the prime minister, Law is the most powerful man in England. Kipling roars and rages like a wounded tiger. His friend Bonar Law stands before him with his head bowed. The distraught maid puts her hands over her ears and runs out of the room.

A fourth door flies open. Carrie Kipling storms in.

"Darling!" she calls, looking around anxiously. Her husband becomes quiet all of a sudden. "It's John, isn't it? News about John?"

"Carrie, I am very sorry," Mr. Law mutters.

"Is he?" She already knows the terrible answer; it is clear by the anguished look on her face.

"Missing. Not quite a week ago," the politician says with a sigh. "Last Monday, September 27, in a battle at Loos."

Rudyard Kipling is silent as he stares blankly at the ceiling. Carrie snatches the telegram from his chair.

"'Missing in action,'" she reads. "My God!" She maintains her composure. "Is there a chance, do you think that he . . . ?"

Mr. Law shakes his head carefully. "We must hope and pray," he whispers hoarsely.

"John, my boy!" Rudyard's voice is as dry as parchment.

"Naturally the War Office informed us immediately," says Mr. Law in a soft, smooth voice, but the rigid, formal undertone of the statesman rings through. "I didn't want the postman to bring you—"

"Of course. Thank you. We appreciate your concern, Mr. Law."

Bateman's is quieter than usual. The Kiplings cling to a single word: "missing." They know all about the scenario with the dreaded telegram, however. Many of their acquaintances have received such messages during the past months. The entire home front lives in fear. Any unexpected knock on the door makes the blood run cold. Every British doorbell is a death knell. Each courier could be the bearer of bad news. Is he bringing word about your husband, your son, a brother, cousin, or friend? Families await the mail in terror.

The Kiplings know all these stories. Most of them end badly, too: Oscar Hornung, the Grenfell brothers, George Cecil and his friend, John Manners. The list is getting longer all the time, just like the daily list of the dead in the newspapers that everyone sifts through. But John? No, their boy doesn't belong in that group. It's impossible. Not yet.

Rudyard Kipling is like a beaten dog. He sits silently upstairs in his writing room, unable to concentrate on anything. He has just returned from France and is suffering from a bad cold. If only he had received this shattering news during his visit to the front! Perhaps he could have organized something. Now he locks himself away, talks to no one, and waits patiently. And he knows that Carrie is feeling the same way downstairs. And John's poor sister, Elsie, too. They are sick with doubt and grief.

Why doesn't Rudyard get his powerful friends involved? Can't he start searching for his son himself?

No one would deny him a travel pass if he wanted to return to France right away. But no, not now. Is he afraid that more news about John is forthcoming?

His thick, bristly mustache hides clenched teeth. His left hand unconsciously rubs his aching stomach—a new tic. The lively, steel-blue eyes are now dull and sunken behind the ever-present glasses. The writer sits at his cluttered table. It is from this spot that he has treated the world to breathtaking adventures. Now he peers wearily through his thick lenses and stares out the window and across the quiet little street. Donkey Hill is an empty pasture. The animals are in the stable. The crown on the large oak tree is turning brown. The clock strikes the time in the hall.

Once again Rudyard Kipling lets his gaze fall on the sheet of paper under his fingers. It's the last letter from his son, which came the day before the fatal telegram. He has read John's words backwards and forwards, probably ten or twenty times.

> *We are very wet and tired. Finally we're lying in the*
> *straw. I can't sleep with this pounding headache. Too*
> *tired, I think. This is another very hurried line as we*

start off tonight. Everyone knows the order: be ready to move at 30 minutes' notice. The frontline trenches are nine miles off from here so it won't be a very long march.

Rudyard Kipling tries to picture his only son: exhausted, wet, anxious about the trial by fire. What was going through his boy's mind the night before he disappeared?

This is THE great effort to break through and end the war. We have to push through at all costs. We'll be in the trenches and therefore will have little time for writing. Funny to think one will be in the thick of it tomorrow. This is a fantastic adventure! But what a responsibility, too. They are staking a tremendous lot on this great advancing movement as if it succeeds the war won't go on for long. You have no idea what enormous issues depend on the next few days.

Rudyard analyzes the sheet of paper, word by word; it is as though he wants to hear a voice, feel a breath.

This will be my last letter most likely for some time as

we won't get any time for writing this next week.
Well, so long old dears.
Dear love,
John

■ ■ ■

Three days pass without further news. It is October 5, 1915, and the helpless feeling from just waiting around is becoming unbearable. Rudyard and Carrie set out in their Rolls-Royce for the Irish Guards' headquarters in London. There they meet with Viscount de Vesci, a senior officer. In spite of his excellent connections, the viscount knows even less about John's disappearance than the Kiplings do. Rudyard and Carrie are disillusioned, but the wheels have been set in motion; instead of waiting around like frightened rabbits, they will undertake the investigation themselves. And those who have important friends — as the Kiplings do — can open doors.

On this same day they visit Max Aitken in Leatherhead, where they spent Christmas night with John. Sir Max is just back from France and was informed that the young Kipling had been wounded and left behind in or near a little building that was surrounded by Germans a few minutes later. There are no further details. John's commander, Colonel Butler, added that Lieutenant Kipling was wounded on an open field where he lay with his men. Only nine of them returned.

The next day all the papers report the news. Anything about Kipling is news.

> *Mr. John Kipling was the boy for whom his famous father wrote the* Just So Stories, *the child for whom Puck told so many immortal stories from the beloved land.*

Rudyard and Carrie don't mention it, but they also read the words "Missing, believed killed." At least the telegram left a glimmer of hope with "Missing in action." Their hearts bleed as they read the article by the journalist Gwynne, Rudyard's good friend:

> *The Kiplings are paying the highest price: their only son. Yet they could have avoided this sad fate in view of their boy's young age and frail health. In spite of*

everything, John wanted to do his part in the war. The whole British Empire sympathizes with Mr. and Mrs. Kipling.

It's not exactly a comforting thought for Rudyard, who did everything he could to send a Kipling to the front.

The small post office in Burwash is flooded with letters. Sympathy cards flow into Bateman's by the thousand. Many letters arrive from acquaintances in the highest circles, even from the former president Theodore Roosevelt, who will also lose a son in the war some time later. Sir John French, field marshall in the British Expeditionary Force, sends a telegram:

THE TERRAIN WHERE JOHN DISAPPEARED HAS BEEN RECAPTURED. PERHAPS WE'LL FIND A TRACE.

At the time he receives the telegram, Rudyard learns that Lieutenant Rupert Grayson, John's best friend at the front, was also wounded on September 27, the day in question. In the same attack, too. Grayson is back in

England. Rudyard and Carrie Kipling leave immediately for the hospital to speak with the young man, even though they are aware that he won't be able to tell them very much. Rupert is recovering from a concussion and some minor wounds he received after being blown into the air by a shell. He can only remember a few small things, including the excitement on the night before the attack. John's parents are warmed by the thought that Rupert was with John in his last hours. And Rupert has a tip for them, too. Edward, Prince of Wales, is a member of the staff of Lord Cavan, commander of the Guards Division. The prince is a popular figure who can move freely at the front. Rupert sends him a telegram and asks if he can find out more about Lieutenant Kipling.

The prince sends his personal answer a few days later. He went to the scene, did all he could, but has come to the same conclusion as Captain Bird. And Prince Edward feels terrible that he can't do more for the Kipling family.

Rudyard and Carrie know who Captain Bird is. On September 26 and 27, he conveyed the order to attack to the John's Second Company. On October 11, two weeks after John's disappearance, the Kiplings receive the classic letter that is sent to all parents or spouses of a fallen soldier. But Bird's letter goes beyond the call of duty; he writes that John was leading a platoon in the direction of Pit 14. A red brick building was standing there. They lay under heavy machine-gun fire. Two of Bird's men noticed that John was limping and then fell near the building. They say someone ran toward him to help. Perhaps it was his orderly, a personal aide that is assigned to each officer. Later this orderly appeared to be missing, as well. Captain Bird hopes that Lieutenant Kipling is alive and a prisoner of war.

Word about John diminishes, but the Kiplings grasp at any straw. Almost every day the Royal Navy's hospital ships bring the newly wounded from Belgium and France to the army hospitals in southern England. Some of those wounded are Irish Guards who fought in the Battle of Loos. On October 26, a month after the battle, Rudyard and Carrie are at the bedside of Private Troy in the Eastern General Hospital at Brighton. Troy clearly remembers that first attack on the Monday when Lieutenant Kipling was wounded. He recalls how they crept through Chalk Pit Wood and fell under enemy fire, which was coming from the direction of a house standing on the left and several mine buildings on the right.

Carrie is sitting on the edge of her chair; Rudyard is diligently jotting down the account in a small notebook.

"It was a two-storied house," the private says. "And it was full of Germans."

"Was Lieutenant Kipling in the area?" Rudyard wants to know. "Did you see him?"

"Oh yes, and how! The lieutenant stormed the building, even though there were machine guns set up inside. And he fired his revolver into the windows. He must have killed a few Germans, sir, that's for sure!"

"Was he wounded?"

"I heard later that he was badly wounded in the neck."

"Who told you that?" Carrie asks in disbelief.

"Sorry, Mrs. Kipling, I don't remember. He was okay when I saw him attack the house. That was the last I saw of him. Your son was a brave officer, believe me. And so good to his men. He would regularly buy bread and tea for us, and even paper so that we could write home. Even though not all of us could write. But sometimes he wrote letters for us."

They are pleasing words for the parents, and Rudyard is especially satisfied because Troy's description is exactly the same as those of other witnesses. The places he describes tally perfectly with the detail map of the battlefield, too. But that injury to John's neck is probably a fabrication, Rudyard thinks.

His hope is short-lived. In November the Red Cross sends the Kiplings a report from Sergeant Kinneally, Fourth Company, Second Battalion Irish Guards:

> *Then I came on Lieutenant Packenham-Law, who was dead, and then met Sergeant Cole, also of the Fourth Company. He said, "Poor Mr. Kipling is killed." Then I came on Mr. Kipling myself. He was lying on his face and his head was covered with blood. I am sure that he was then dead. This must have been about an hour after he was hit. At that moment we were being heavily shelled . . .*
>
> *It would not have been possible for Lieutenant Kipling to have been taken prisoner. The whole Guards Division was between the Germans and the place where he lay, and we have held the ground ever since.*

"This report can't be right," Carrie Kipling protests,

and in the margin she writes, "Quite incorrect." But Sergeant Kinneally has more bad news:

> *I can easily explain why his body was not found and brought in. The ground where he lay was very heavily shelled by the big guns, and men lying there might be buried in a crater. It was impossible to bring in even all the wounded men, let alone the dead.*

Another letter arrives a day later. It is from Sergeant Cochrane, who has sent Rudyard an extensive eyewitness account from the Red Cross Hospital in Springburn. He knew John well and fought alongside him on September 27. Cochrane was in the sixth platoon, situated next to the fifth platoon that John led, but in the confusion of the advance the two groups merged into one.

> *On Sunday 26 September we marched to Vermelles, our first stop at the front, near Loos. The day before we sloshed through the rain for 15 hours and it was only late in the night that we found a place to sleep.*

This time Captain Alexander and Captain Hubbard walked in front to scout out the trenches that we were to take over from our fellow soldiers, the First Scots Guards. There was much confusion when we arrived. Our officers had a long discussion with the Scots. Who was going to do what? It was eventually decided that we Irish Guards would occupy the trenches that had been captured from the Germans, which lay in a line between Le Rutoire and Lone Tree. Just before midnight we reached our positions, dead tired once again. Two or three hours later came the command to move 500 meters to the east. It was already growing light when we finally sat at our firing line. Our trench was close to the road that ran from Loos to Hulluch.

At about four o'clock we left our positions and slowly began to advance. My platoon was next to Lieutenant Kipling's, but our men got mixed together rather quickly and Lieutenant Kipling took charge of the two platoons. There was shooting exchanged with the enemy. He kept walking to and fro along our line. I politely advised him to lie down and share the protection of my sandbag, but he waved the advice away with a laugh. Then a German machine gun began to plow into our area. I pulled Mr. Kipling down by his sleeve. It was just in time, for our sandbags were hit. He didn't appear frightened at all. "Quite warm here, isn't it, Sergeant!" he said, and he laughed. The order to attack came after that. Lieutenant Kipling led the charge and ran in front to the first buildings near the chalk pit. We could get closer to them by going through a gap in the wall that surrounded the grounds. We made our way through the piles of rubbish in the yard. He and I got very near to the window from where the machine gun was firing. The lieutenant sidled along the wall so that the Germans could not hit him without exposing themselves. He took his pistol and fired inside. Others in the meantime smashed the door in. We cleaned up the machine-gun nest. There were about 25 Germans in it. We killed them all.

I was hit by a bullet near the building, but I didn't even feel it in the heat of battle. When the mine buildings had been cleaned up, Mr. Kipling called out, "Come on, boys!" We rushed round the right of the house, where some of our other men were. We went on immediately to the first German trench, which ran along a line about 30 meters behind the pit building. Then I was hit again. Later it appeared that I had been grazed by a lead ball from a fragmentation shell, a piece of shrapnel. I fell and the others went on, led and encouraged by Lieutenant Kipling. They dove into a wood behind the German trench. That was the last I saw of Mr. Kipling. Nor have I heard from any of our men what happened to him afterwards.

Our regiment and another division cleared out this wood the next day and found our dead. Since they did not find Lieutenant Kipling, it is possible that he was wounded and taken prisoner. Otherwise I would have expected his body to be found. As an officer he was rather conspicuous, with an officer's cap and a leather Sam Browne belt (our belts are made of cloth).

I lay there for 24 hours, even during the German counterattack. Shells were falling all around me. It's a miracle I survived. I was finally able to get back to my own lines by rolling myself along the ground. I was then taken to a dressing station near Hulluch.

■ ■ ■

Rudyard and Carrie draw additional strength from the letter. John was a brave, capable officer and a good human being, too. His soldiers respected him. And above all, once again there are some signs indicating that their son might still be alive.

■   ■   ■

The months crawl by. The war continues unabated, but in the Kipling home it stopped on September 27, 1915. Rudyard and his wife hear little more about their lost son. On the field there is not a trace of John to be seen. Carrie takes her mind off her troubles by making Red Cross packages, which are sent to the boys at the front. Elsie sews and mends clothes for the wounded, and sends gifts to them. She is the chauffeur for the family now and drives *Car-Uso*, her brother's Singer. And while of course Rudyard is still known as the famous writer, the Nobel Prize winner, his pen dries up. His thoughts become somber. He gets sick more often and constantly has stomach complaints. There are no more exciting adventures, there is no Puck or Mowgli. Rudyard waits impatiently for a sign of his son, his own Mowgli, dead or alive. And every day the question running through his head becomes clearer: *Why? Did he have to defend that war so strongly?* Who dies if England live? *What kind of a father sends his only son to his death? How many boys have I written into the grave,* he wonders.

On a dark day he seizes upon his doubt and bitterness and expresses them in two lines:

> *If any question why we died,*
> *Tell them, because our fathers lied.*

The Kiplings get a new lead every now and then. They continue to believe that John is a prisoner of war in a German camp. Through Lady Edward, they have contact with Margaret, Crown Princess of Sweden. Even though the princess has family ties to the German Kaiser, her efforts to find John are to no avail.

In 1917, two years after John's death, Rudyard arranges for an airplane to drop a load of fliers over the German lines. Written in German, these fliers ask for news about his son, for Rudyard still firmly believes that John has been wounded and the Germans are waiting for him to recover. The captured son of a world-famous father would be an invaluable figure to flaunt for propaganda purposes. But the fliers garner no response.

There is silence on the official side as well. Rudyard's powerful friends in government, at court, and in the army have other worries besides finding John Kipling, and they certainly have more dead. The toll is horrific; when the First World War ends on November 11, 1918, the British alone can count more than a million lost sons. The worldwide death count is twenty times that. John Kipling was just one small officer in the Great War.

THE LOST SON

RUDYARD KIPLING IS SITTING AT HIS DESK, DREAMING AWAY. THE OLD writer's shaggy mustache covers up a sharp twist on his tense lips. His left hand rubs his aching stomach. He has acquired many nervous tics. Tired eyes look out the window at the mighty oaks on Donkey Hill and the little meadow in front of the house. Rudyard is thinking about John, his son. Who else?

Rudyard dozes off. Mowgli appears before him: the man-cub from *The Jungle Book*, that other child of his who grew up with wolves. Mowgli always reminds him of John.

KIPLING. War is worse, Mowgli. Worse than the jungle.

MOWGLI. Do you think so, Mr. Kipling?

KIPLING. The front in France doesn't let go of its prey, Mowgli. The monster has an insatiable hunger.

MOWGLI. Worse than Shere Khan, the tiger?

KIPLING. And meaner than Tabaqui, that sly, sneaky jackal.

MOWGLI. That's terrible, Mr. Kipling.

KIPLING. Will *you* be my son, Mowgli?

MOWGLI. But I'm the man-cub sir. The man-cub has no father or mother. And *you* are Rudyard Kipling, the world-famous writer!

KIPLING. My son has disappeared in the jungle. My only son!

MOWGLI. Isn't there any trace at all?

KIPLING. Nothing.

MOWGLI. Not a hair, not a bone? *(Silence.)* I'm very sorry, sir.

KIPLING. Daddo, that's what he used to call me.

MOWGLI. Daddo. *(Silence.)*

KIPLING. I sent you into the jungle, Mowgli. Just like that.

MOWGLI. I was a young tenderfoot then, inexperienced and naive.

KIPLING. But *you* survived, Mowgli. John didn't.

MOWGLI. That's terrible, Mr. Kipling — Daddo.

KIPLING. You survived without a father. Now I must survive without a son, my son.

EPILOGUE

AMONG THE MANY HONORS, AWARDS, AND NOBLE TITLES THAT WERE OFFERED to him, Rudyard Kipling accepted only the academic or literary ones. Because of his widespread popularity, from a fairly young age he was regularly asked to join the boards of prestigious societies and foundations. He invariably declined these offers. Thus it is noteworthy that in 1917 he agreed to serve on the Imperial War Graves Commission, which was established by royal decree in that same year. Now known as the Commonwealth War Graves Commission, it is still very active in 150 countries all over the world. There are 2,500 cemeteries and countless monuments dedicated to the hundreds of thousands of fallen soldiers from all the countries of the British Commonwealth. Kipling wanted to do something for John, his only son. And he undoubtedly took on this mission to make amends for all those many other lost sons. Rudyard Kipling was the official author of innumerable inscriptions. He furnished the texts that are carved on large and small war monuments. One of those texts is unique:

We run across the text in every big British military cemetery all over the world. It is inscribed on the Stone of Remembrance, which looks a bit like an altar. As always, Kipling's thoughts were of John when he came up with this inscription. The inspiration was from an obscure Bible fragment in the Apocrypha (Ecclesiasticus, Jesus Sirach 44:9–14). Kipling used just the last line, but the lines preceding it totally reflect his bitterness over John's disappearance:

BUT THERE ARE A FEW FOR WHOM THERE IS NO REMEMBRANCE,

AND THEY PERISH AS THOUGH THEY HAD NEVER EXISTED,

AS IF THEY HAD NEVER BEEN BORN.

In the summer of 1920, Kipling combined one of his regular vacations to France with his work for the Imperial War Graves Commission. Together with Carrie, he toured the battlefields. They visited Loos, taking with them maps and notes from their interviews of soldiers. They found nothing.

A year later they organized one last systematic search

in the same area. The Kiplings hoped for a small miracle. Once again their efforts were fruitless.

In 1922, Rudyard accompanied King George V and Queen Mary on their pilgrimage to the battlefields. They rode through Vlamertinge, Ypres, and Poperinge, and they visited the Somme Valley. From there Rudyard continued on alone to Loos. This time he was bowled over by the changes there. "The road, the area where John disappeared, Chalk Pit and Red House . . . are so smoothed out that they are unrecognizable," he noted, disillusioned.

The trails had been wiped out. There was absolutely no hope of finding John.

On August 4, 1930, Rudyard and Carrie traveled to France together one last time. They attended the dedication of the Loos Memorial. Inscribed on a long wall at Dud Corner Cemetery were the names of countless British soldiers who died in the area but had no grave. One name carved in the wall received their special attention: Lieutenant John Kipling.

In 1992, the inspectors of the War Graves Commission made a very peculiar discovery: The body of an unknown lieutenant in the Irish Guards buried at the Saint Mary's

Dressing Station in Haisnes (near Loos) is that of the eighteen-year-old John Kipling. Even though some doubted the truth of this discovery, the gravestone finally got a name.

But by this time Rudyard Kipling had been dead for years. He had passed away in 1936, a broken man.

BIBLIOGRAPHY

Holt, Tonie and Valmai. *My Boy Jack?* Yorkshire:
Pen & Sword Books, 1998.

Lycett, Andrew. *Rudyard Kipling.* London:
Weidenfeld & Nicolson, 1999.